AN U
CROWN

The Tudor Saga Series
Book Four

David Field

SAPERE
BOOKS

AN UNEASY CROWN

Published by Sapere Books.

11 Bank Chambers, Hornsey, London, N8 7NN,
United Kingdom

saperebooks.com

ISBN: 978-1-913335-23-6

I

Two little girls, giggling hysterically, rolled and tumbled down the gentle slope from the stables of Bradgate House. They were wearing the 'play' smocks that Nanny Calthorpe had insisted on, out of an abundance of caution, but they would still be in serious disgrace when eventually obliged to show themselves to her.

Of the two girls, Grace was by far the muddier as their wild career down the grassy slope came to a natural end when they reached the fishpond.

'Let's go and look at the carp!' Jane suggested and Grace needed no persuasion.

They scampered to the muddy edge of the natural water-filled hollow, their bare feet squelching deliciously as they felt the cool ooze welling up between their toes in relief against the cloudless heat of an August sky. They had just begun to compete with each other as to which of them could spy the most fish when a stern voice with which they were both only too familiar boomed down at them from the top of the slope.

'Get out of there immediately, you naughty girls! We must get you cleaned up and changed without delay! The guests have arrived and your fathers will beat you if they see the state you've got your clothing into. Up here — now!'

Jane and Grace sighed and extracted their feet from the slime with a sucking noise that invoked more giggles, then trotted dutifully back up the slope under the stern glare of Nanny Calthorpe.

Although she was now well over sixty, Mary Calthorpe had lost none of the formidable authority with which she had once presided over a small convent of Benedictine nuns as 'Mother Mary Magdalena', before the house had been closed on the order of the former Master Secretary, Thomas Cromwell. Mary had been allowed to continue her work within the local community, thanks to the kindness and foresight of the Lord of the Manor of Knighton, Sir Richard Ashton, on whose estate the former convent had stood.

Knighton lay half a day's ride to the south of Bradgate House and Mary Calthorpe's natural skill in healing had led Sir Richard to choose her to assist in the delivery of his daughter, Grace, four years previously. Mary had then been employed as wet-nurse and governess at Bradgate House for the slightly elder girl, Jane Grey. Though Mary was officially only governess to Jane, she performed a similar service to Grace, who was Jane's constant companion.

Jane Grey, now aged five, was the daughter of Henry Grey, Marquess of Dorset and Lady Frances, who in turn was niece of King Henry VIII, through the marriage of his sister to Charles Brandon, Duke of Suffolk. By virtue of this family connection, Jane's father had once been regularly at Court, but for all his honours and high esteem Henry Grey was at heart a simple man who preferred his country estate in Leicestershire to the noise and intrigue of life at the Court of Henry VIII.

Henry Grey had grown close to Richard Ashton, and the two men had been happy to allow their two girls to grow up as companions, given that they were the only two daughters of wealth for miles around. But the 'wealth' of their two estates was sharply contrasted. Whereas Bradgate ran into hundreds of acres, with a river, a deer park, an ornamental garden of sorts and several fishponds surrounding the substantial many-roomed brick and timber house towards its southern boundary,

Sir Richard Ashton's manor of Knighton was far more modest, despite his lineage.

Richard Ashton came by direct descent from the so-called 'usurper' Perkin Warbeck, who he had been told had in reality been the long-lost Duke of York, one of the believed murdered 'Princes in the Tower'. This had been revealed to Richard Ashton by his mentor Thomas Cromwell, Master Secretary to King Henry, whose life had ended on the scaffold two years previously. Had it not been for the victory of the first Tudor, Henry of Richmond, at Bosworth, only a few hours ride from Bradgate, Richard Ashton would have become in due course the rightful King of England.

Cromwell had used this fact to manipulate Ashton into acting as his spy at the Court, then presided over by Anne Boleyn. Information supplied by Ashton to Cromwell, while carrying out a very secondary role as one of his clerks, had led Anne to the executioner, but not before Ashton had met and bedded Anne's sister-in-law Jane, Lady Rochford, who had borne him a daughter — Grace. Jane Rochford had then returned to the intrigue of Court in time to meet her death on Tower Green on the same day as the most recent of Henry's queens, Catherine Howard. Richard Ashton, meanwhile, had fallen for and taken to wife, Mary Calthorpe's own niece, Kate Calthorpe.

Ashton had seen enough of life at the Tudor Court to want none of it, but he had, as 'Cromwell's man', made an implacable enemy of Thomas Howard, Duke of Norfolk, and he lived with the ever-present, if slowly diminishing, fear that Norfolk was not yet done with him. He therefore relied heavily on the protection of his near neighbour Henry Grey, whose father-in-law Charles Brandon, the Duke of Suffolk, was

Norfolk's enemy at Court, where the two men competed for volume in King Henry's ear.

Both neighbouring families were awaiting the latest news from Court from Edward Seymour, Earl of Hertford, brother of the late Queen, Jane Seymour and uncle to the infant heir Edward. Edward Seymour and his wife, Anne, had arrived at Bradgate House only an hour previously, with their entourage in tow.

The two girls shivered their penance as Mary Calthorpe doused each of them with a pail of cold water and began scrubbing them vigorously with a rough cloth, ignoring their howls of pain and their pleas for mercy. Then they climbed into their best gowns and submitted with gritted teeth to the tugging out of their hair. Grace had taken the dark auburn hair colouring of the birth mother she had never really known, whereas for Jane it was the ubiquitous red that was seemingly the legacy of every Tudor, and in her case came from her royal grandmother the Princess Mary, King Henry's late younger sister.

Suitably cleansed and robed, Jane and Grace were led into the Great Hall by a stern-faced Mary Calthorpe and told to sit at the small table to the side which, as always, was reserved for them. At the centre of the head table sat the banquet host Henry Grey, with his wife Lady Frances to his left. To his right sat Edward Seymour with his wife, and beyond him Richard Ashton and his young bride Kate, only some two months away from giving birth herself.

The guest of honour, Edward Seymour, moved his seat next to Ashton's, in order to bring him up to date with affairs in London. Seymour and Ashton had formed a natural friendship when the Seymours had been elevated from their humble Wiltshire estate by the marriage of their oldest daughter, Jane to King Henry. Jane had been a lady-in-waiting to the former Queen Anne, who had bullied and belittled her openly during her daily audiences. As a young clerk, Richard Ashton, sent into the royal presence by his master Cromwell, had been one of the few to befriend Jane and after a while had given her the courage to accept Henry's hand in marriage.

The Seymours had remained forever grateful for this kindness and even after Jane's tragic death, following the birth of Prince Edward, they had smiled favourably on 'Sir' Richard Ashton, as he had been knighted by an equally grateful King Henry. Edward Seymour had also bathed in the warm glow from the throne and now bore the titles of Viscount Beauchamp and Earl of Hertford. He was also Warden of the Scottish Marches and it was in this capacity that he was riding north at the head of an army.

'I had not been aware that we were at war with the Scots,' Ashton admitted to Seymour as he peeled a plum, 'although, of course, I have long been absent from Court, for reasons of which you will be only too aware.'

'You need no longer fear Norfolk,' Seymour assured him, 'since he seems reconciled with Henry of late and therefore will not risk creating any further ructions in Council. With Cromwell gone, Norfolk seems of late to have lost some of his bile.'

'That is something for which to be grateful,' Ashton replied, 'and I thank you for that happy intelligence. But why the armed progress into Scotland?'

'Henry's real wish is to invade France,' Seymour continued. 'But, as ever, he is conscious of Scotland at his northern boundary, eager to create difficulties as part of its long-lasting understanding with France. As you may be aware, Francis of France and Charles of Spain are at each other's throats once more, and Henry has concluded a secret alliance with Charles, one of the terms of which is that he will invade France. He has delayed doing so and has finally been shamed into undertaking an invasion next year. But he wishes to guard his back door, hence his orders to me to ride north with an army and remind King James that any nonsense from him will result in the most serious consequences for his nation.'

'Surely as Henry's nephew by marriage, the Scottish King will be happy to oblige?'

Seymour frowned. 'James will shortly be delivered of an heir through his wife Mary of Guise, which further strengthens Scotland's unofficial alliance with France. His mother — Henry's sister — died late last year and there is no longer anyone north of the rather uncertain and lawless border to argue for an enduring peace with England.'

Mary Calthorpe had been hovering a few feet away, respectfully awaiting the opportunity to speak to Sir Richard. Richard Ashton beckoned her over with a smile and introduced her to Edward Seymour.

'This is the Earl of Hertford, Mary. He rides north in a few days to put the Scots in their place. Edward, this is my daughter Grace's nurse and taskmistress, although she is officially employed as governess to the Lady Jane and her younger sister the Lady Catherine. But since Jane and Grace are inseparable, Mary discharges duties in respect of them all. She is the finest governess and nurse I could wish for.'

Edward Seymour nodded formally to Mary, who blushed, curtsied, then turned to address Richard Ashton. 'Begging your pardon, Master, but will you require Mistress Grace to be prepared for travel shortly? She has dined and grows restless and should it be your intention to return to Knighton today, then I shall needs be required to hold on to her by the neck of her gown, ere she slips out into more mischief with the Lady Jane.'

Richard chuckled lightly and nodded. 'Indeed, we shall be riding back to Knighton long before the sun begins its descent, if we are to be assured of reaching it by dark, so please ensure that my daughter does not leave the hall.'

As Mary bowed backwards and slipped away with her instructions, Edward Seymour followed her progress down the hall with his eyes and nodded to where the two young girls were in animated conversation.

'You are most fortunate in having a suitable companion for your daughter so close at hand.'

'They are far too friendly,' Ashton chuckled, 'and a thoroughly bad influence, the one upon the other. Although Jane is almost a year older than Grace, she is somewhat strictly governed in her upbringing, in consequence of which she tends to celebrate the more freely when she is released into Grace's company. The two of them can be relied upon to leave the house appropriately clad in clean garments, only to return — whenever their hiding places can be discovered — looking like scarecrows from the field. Mary is forever demanding that I chastise Grace, but somehow I fail in that simple task whenever I look into her eyes and she gives me that whimsical smile so full of love and childish innocence.'

Seymour laughed and nodded. 'It is, I think, the fate of all fathers to be in thrall to small daughters. I have three of my own, one of whom is little older than your Grace, and whenever her mother calls upon me to administer the rod, I cannot bring myself to do it if I look first into her little face.'

'I hope to fare better should Kate bear me a son in a few weeks,' Ashton said as he nodded towards his wife, still deep in conversation with the Countess Anne.

'Grace is not Kate's daughter, I believe?'

'Indeed she is not,' Ashton confirmed, 'for all the difference it makes to Grace, who has never known any other mother. Her birth mother went to the scaffold along with the last Queen. Hopefully the days are now past when vile intrigues at Court can make such things possible. Has the King shown any interest in further marriage?'

Edward Seymour looked round carefully before lowering his voice in reply. 'No, and after the last two, who can blame him? But in truth, apart from his crown he is no great prospect — not as he once was, anyway. He grows fatter by the day, but will not exercise and his face has lost that healthy glow of the athlete and soldier that was wont to set him apart from other men — that and his height, and even that seems to diminish as his width swells to compete with it. His ulcerous wound also creates a permanent and disagreeable smell about him. All in all, he needs a nurse more than he needs a wife, and I suspect that he knows that.'

'Very sad indeed,' Ashton nodded. 'And now, if we can separate our wives, I must make preparations to depart. Do you stay here the night?'

'Several nights, probably,' Seymour replied, 'since it is the last chance that Anne and I will have to sleep together in comfort. Once I rejoin my men we must recommence the northern march, while my wife will ride back under escort to our estate in Sussex, where our children await her return.'

'One of the hardships of being a successful soldier,' Ashton observed. 'I have rarely lifted a sword, even for exercise, and I do not intend to do so ever again, since it would cause Kate so much anguish were I to be away in battle, with no certainty that I would return.'

'Yet there is no shortage of men prepared to hazard such risks,' Seymour reminded him. 'Even that old warhorse Norfolk, who one would have expected to hang up his armour and weaponry years ago, is champing at the bit to be the one to lead Henry's forces into France. In that he is opposed by Suffolk, who is no younger than Norfolk by any great measure. They are held in check by King Henry, who — God help us — still commands his armourer to forge new and more costly armour for him to wear at the head of his army. I pity the poor horse condemned to carry that lot on its back.'

II

'When may I see the baby?' Grace demanded excitedly as a weary Mary Calthorpe brought the good news downstairs at Knighton.

'When your father says you may,' Mary replied sternly. 'Even he has not seen him yet.'

'Is Kate sleeping now?' Richard Ashton enquired from his seat in the corner, wine mug in hand.

'Yes, Master,' Mary replied. 'It was not the easiest laying-in I have attended, but neither was it the worst, and Baby Thomas is being bathed and wrapped as we speak.'

Grace had wandered over to where her father sat and as she eased herself into a standing position between his knees she looked up at him with her dark eyes set in the pleading expression that she had never known to fail. 'Father, when you go up, may I go with you? He's my baby brother and I want to hold him.'

Ashton smiled lovingly, leaned forward and ruffled her untidy dark locks with his free hand. 'Come on then — let's go and see.'

Susan Lilybank smiled shyly as she handed Ashton the snuffling bundle, relieved to be free of the unaccustomed responsibility of holding something so small and defenceless. 'He's already fed at the breast, Master, and I've cleaned him up. The Mistress is sleeping soundly.'

'Thank you, Susan,' Ashton replied with a gentle smile. 'You've done very well and Mary speaks highly of your assistance. Now perhaps you need to go and rest.'

'Yes, Master. Thank you kindly.' The girl curtsied as she scuttled for the narrow staircase.

Richard Ashton looked down at the bundle in his arms, blowing mucus bubbles by way of their first introduction, then he lowered it so that Grace could peer into the swaddling.

She frowned. 'Why are his eyes closed?'

'He's sleeping.'

'He looks like a mole, or a rat.'

Ashton chuckled. 'Best not say that when he grows to manhood,' he told her, 'or he might box your ears.'

'If he does, I'll get my husband to run him through,' the little girl replied innocently.

Ashton froze. 'Do you know what that means, Grace?'

'No, but Jane says that's what gentlemen do at Court.'

'Then perhaps you should stay away from Court, as I do.'

There was a faint stirring from the bed and Grace rushed over and, to Richard Ashton's horror, leapt straight onto the rousing form.

'Get off there now!' Ashton commanded her and as she rolled sideways he hurried over and apologised as he took Kate's limp and coldly sweating hand. 'He's beautiful — thank you.'

'Thank Aunt Mary for her skills and tender care,' Kate replied hoarsely. 'It was quite difficult near the end, but she seemed to know where to press and then Thomas just seemed to slide out easily. We did agree to call him "Thomas", didn't we?'

'Yes, we did, after the man who brought me from obscurity into the world where I met you. And, of course, for the Cardinal who first placed his feet on the road to wealth and fortune.'

'And then the road to Tower Hill,' Kate reminded him. 'Please God that our Thomas doesn't go down that road.'

Further north, the battle between England and Scotland was over almost as soon as it began. For King James, it was the final blow. He had lost his royal battle standard and his most experienced commander in the field. He withdrew to Falkland Palace, humiliated and racked by fever, only to be informed that Mary of Guise had given birth to a daughter bearing her name, rather than the son that James had been eagerly anticipating. His resistance to natural disease lowered even further by his depleted spirit, he died two weeks later at the age of thirty, leaving Scotland in the hands of a girl barely two weeks old.

Some of the higher born Scots prisoners were well cared for, in a gesture of magnanimity by King Henry, who had hopes of using them to convey good reports back to their fellow nobles who dominated the Regency of the Princess Mary of Scotland. In particular, the more elevated of them were invited to partake of the massive Christmas Day feast at Hampton Court Palace that was being hosted by the Lady Mary and graced by her Ladies. It had been left to one of them, Lady Catherine Parr, to devise the masques in association with Edward Seymour's brother, Thomas.

Late in the afternoon on Christmas Day, as the trestles were reloaded with platters of fruits and sweets and the serving girls scuttled back to the Buttery for refills of their wine jugs, the diversions commenced. Acrobats and jugglers passed between the long tables, exploiting their talents in return for coin, while the musicians in the gallery struck up with light-hearted madrigals and folk songs to cause the assembled company to rejoice in their Englishness. Soon there would be dancing, but at the far side of the Banqueting Hall the stage was being set for the main masque of the day.

There was a brief fanfare and Thomas Seymour entered, wearing a red gown and with Devil's horns on his head. He gave a sweeping bow and in a commanding voice he addressed the assembled company, with particular attention to King Henry, who was already well into his cups and leaning backwards in his chair in what was often the prelude to his falling asleep. Thomas Seymour was determined that this would not occur while he was in command of the revels.

'My noble lords and ladies,' he bellowed, 'welcome to the Land of Misrule, where Gluttony, Pride and Lust have proved to be the Devil's handmaidens and reduced the land to misery and despair.'

With an imperious wave he beckoned in the first of the silent mummers, recognisable members of the King's Court, but draped in costumes appropriate to the roles they were playing. First came Gluttony, a grotesquely fat human egg of gigantic proportions, tottering on spindly legs and seemingly chewing on an oversized haunch of meat that was twice even its own size, before it fell flat on its back and wriggled its legs in the air, prior to being carted off, protesting, by four servers dressed in royal livery.

Next came Pride, dressed in an outlandish outfit that glittered with obvious fake jewels, mincing up and down and admiring itself in a massive hand mirror eight feet high. Peals of laughter greeted its humiliating demise, as liveried servers stepped forward with large pails filled with suggestively brown water, which they used in order to drench the character from head to foot. The costume, craftily constructed from thin vellum, collapsed in a soggy mess and revealed a bedraggled wretch clad only in brown shirt and hose, who ran out of the Hall in a pretence of concealing its private parts from public scrutiny, to hysterical cat-calls from the audience.

Finally came Lust, with a grossly exaggerated set of bosoms and face make-up reminiscent of a badly painted Fool. After prancing up and down for several minutes, beckoning invitingly to those watching the proceedings, the character was accosted by two liveried ushers, each armed with a spike on the end of a long pole, which they used to deflate the massive bosoms, revealed to be pigs' bladders filled with water, that emptied with a rude noise as the ushers chased the character out with further menacing thrusts.

As the laughter died down, Thomas Seymour reappeared in a new floor-length costume of pure white, in the manner of an Archbishop's chasuble. He raised his arms for attention and smiled broadly as he revealed the moral of the pageant they had been watching.

'This land has been saved from the horrors of sin by the opening of its arms to the purity of true Faith. As you shall see...' He opened his arms wide in a theatrical gesture and into the Hall rode a figure on a pure white donkey, dressed from head to foot in a white robe and sporting golden wings. On her head was a golden diadem that glistened with clusters of shimmering jewels and in her hand was a battle standard that proudly displayed the lion rampant of England, with Tudor Roses above and below it.

The assembly fell silent as the figure slid from the side saddle and extended her winged arms upwards in a wide arc of blessing. 'I am the beauty of Faith and my arms are forever raised in protection of my loyal children as they follow the path of virtue and light through a world that is beset by wickedness.

Rejoice in the birth day of the Redeemer and live forever in His precious light. And so I take my rest.'

Catherine Parr knelt daintily on one knee and bowed her head, as the applause rang out through the Hall. After at least a minute in this silent pose she raised her hand for Thomas Seymour to take and lead her gently out of the Hall to ongoing applause. Then they re-entered and took a bow, before Thomas led Catherine to where King Henry sat with his daughter, the Lady Mary, at his side.

Henry clapped his hands in appreciation. 'That was well done, Thomas. Well done indeed. And who was your other charming player?'

'This is my newest Lady, Father,' Mary told him. 'She is Catherine Parr, wife of Baron Latimer.'

'She is welcome to Court.' Henry nodded with a welcoming smile. 'Bring her to see me on the morrow.'

Further down the table sat the giant bearded figure of Charles Brandon, Duke of Suffolk, with his Duchess, Catherine.

'Who was the woman playing the part of "Faith"?' the Duchess enquired of her husband.

He belched loudly before replying, 'One of Lady Mary's new clingers-on, I believe. Why do you wish to know?'

'I would wish to make her closer acquaintance,' the Duchess replied. 'She showed courage, putting the old Church in its place like that.'

'Is that what she did?' Suffolk asked disinterestedly.

'Clearly, that was her message. The blind old ways of mumbled Latin, with incense swinging through the air and seats in Heaven to be bought from a priest, now replaced with the purity of God's truth and the dawning of the light on the road to salvation. I'm surprised the Lady Mary let her get away with it, although with that rogue Seymour as master of the revels, it's likely that she had no idea of what was to come.'

'Must you read Reformation messages in everything? So embarrassing when you call out in public and order the "Old Way" to heel.'

'But that is where it belongs, Charles — under the heels of those who truly believe in redemption through the love of Christ and not the intervention of priests. I would meet this brave new Lady whom Henry's pious shrew of a daughter may one day regret having clasped to her bosom.'

Two days later, the King's Council was commanded to assemble and there was only one item for discussion. Following the abject surrender of Scotland's army and the temporary goodwill that Henry had established with those left behind, after the death of King James V, negotiations had been taking place both in London and in Edinburgh regarding the terms upon which the two nations might hopefully learn to live in peace.

Scotland was now under the Regency of the Earl of Arran, ruling on behalf of the tiny girl born less than a month before the recent death of her father. The Princess Mary of Scotland would one day become its Queen, and Henry was hopeful of joining the two crowns for all time with the betrothal of her to his own son, Edward. However, there were voices raised against such a match in Council.

'We would be exposing England to more Reformist heresy,' Stephen Gardiner, Bishop of Winchester argued.

Suffolk saw his chance and jumped in. 'Not all reform is heretical,' he argued with a smirk. 'To assert so is to condemn His Majesty as a heretic.'

'We do not condemn what has hitherto transpired,' Thomas Howard, Duke of Norfolk, argued in defence of the impetuous Gardiner.

Henry raised his hand and it fell silent. 'This has nothing to do with religion,' he argued. 'It has to do, instead, with the peaceful progress of this realm once I am gone. My physicians are wont to lie to me in order, as they see it, to preserve their heads, but I doubt that I have more than a ten year left in me, then the nation will be governed by a young man with no legitimate heirs of his own, unless he be married. My daughters have been excluded from the succession and unless urgent steps are taken to lengthen the direct legitimate line with male heirs, Scotland will inherit England through the descendants of my sister Margaret anyway. Better that we take the initiative and let Scotland marry into England through the male line.'

'We have the Scottish Regent's consent to such a course, Your Majesty,' Edward Seymour replied, 'but it is well known that back in Scotland there are voices against it. There are many who would prefer a match with the Dauphin, to further strengthen the ties between Scotland and France. Strategically we should not let that happen, particularly since it is your intention to lead an army into France when the time is more propitious.'

Henry then turned to the hitherto silent Lord Chancellor, Thomas Wriothesley. 'We can only test the water, Thomas, so draw up the final agreement in terms that will provide for the Princess Mary to live here in England under the wardship of some noble and his wife acceptable to the Regent Arran until her tenth year, at which time she will be allowed a grace and favour estate of her own until the marriage be celebrated. Then present it to Arran in such a way as to advise him that he has no choice and send him home rejoicing.'

'What if our terms are rejected, Your Majesty?' Edward Seymour asked.

Henry smiled unpleasantly. 'Then we shall send you back to Scotland to boot more arses, Edward.'

III

Jane Grey kicked disconsolately at a clump of grass as the two girls wandered through the river meadow, heads down against the squally gale that foreshadowed a spring shower.

'It's always the same when Grandfather Brandon comes to visit,' Jane complained. 'I must stand before them and recite from the Greek or Latin that my tutor has forced me to learn. If I am tardy or resentful, my mother will pinch me until I do it, and then she will make me dance or sing, or take out my latest needlepoint and display it to the company. And my new grandmother will then make comment on how I conduct myself. '

If she was expecting sympathy from Grace, walking sourly by her side, then she was destined to be disappointed. Grace's education thus far had been of the basic sort, conducted by a local priest of whom her parents approved because he performed his religious duties in the English form. But his insistence on teaching in English meant that the mysterious world of the classical scholars was closed to Grace's enquiring mind and she would gladly have changed places with Jane. Not just in order to learn more about what lay in the books that were kept in Jane's schoolroom, but in order to receive tuition in dancing, needlepoint and the playing of musical instruments. Her parents were a simple, honest, straightforward country squire and his devoted wife, and her only other teacher a former nun whose main duties consisted of keeping both her and her friend Jane clean and presentable.

'Why is your grandfather visiting you anyway?' Grace asked.

'He claims that he has something important to ask of my father and he has asked particularly that I be there. I promised to be good if you could be there too, and your father insisted that he be present in order to ensure your good behaviour.'

The two girls presented themselves for dinner in the Great Hall, suitably washed, scrubbed and attired under the stern supervision of Mary Calthorpe, and they were assigned to their usual side table, where they picked petulantly through the range of meats laid on the damask cloths that covered the trestle. Their awareness that they were the object of intense scrutiny from Jane's family guests did nothing to improve their normally small appetites, and Jane in particular was apprehensive and resentful of the fact that once the meal was over, she would be called upon to 'perform'. Grace, for her part, was jealous that Jane would then become the object of everyone's attention.

'She is perfect for the role,' Suffolk told Jane's father as he incised another slice from the home-reared venison on the platter in front of him. 'There are no girls in the royal schoolroom — only a soppy boy called Barnaby whose sole function seems to be to take the cuts when Edward gets something wrong. Given the current state of our relations with Scotland, the proposed betrothal of its baby princess to our prince will come to naught and Edward has no real mind of his own. Nor does he show any inclination to reject choices that are made for him. All we need is for Jane to play the sisterly role at this stage and wait for them to grow fond of each other.'

'And what will be the likely attitude of the royal sisters?' Lady Frances asked.

'Half-sisters only,' Frances was remined by her step-mother, Catherine. 'The Lady Mary is a grown woman and although she is one of Edward's godmothers, there seems to be some distance between them, given her strict observance of the Catholic offices and his inclinations towards the more liberal sciences under the influence of his early tutors. As for Elizabeth, she is still the awkward, headstrong and to my mind far too flighty, baggage that she always was. Yet Edward seems to favour her more than Mary.'

'I think that my wife was enquiring whether or not Jane would be resented by either of the sisters, were she to be introduced into the schoolroom,' Henry Grey intervened.

Catherine shot him a resentful look. 'It will surely be for her to demonstrate, by her learning, that she is a fit companion for a young prince. Their ages are the same and, from what I have been informed, her accomplishments are gently demonstrated and she would provide him with no challenge. Merely sweet friendship that will hopefully mature into something deeper.'

'You ask a great deal of a young girl,' Grey protested.

Catherine smiled sweetly as she took her husband's hand and kissed it. 'It was how dear Charles and I met, when I was his ward. What began as gratitude and warm respect developed into something much more enduring.'

It was all that Henry Grey could do to restrain himself from arguing that it had more to do with Suffolk's notorious lust than anything more paternal or platonic.

Further down the table, Richard and Kate Ashton were exchanging differing predictions as to what might lie in store for their own daughter.

'It will do her no harm to learn more fashionable ways,' Kate was arguing, 'and we are promised that Grace may remain at the Brandon house in London, as a companion to Jane when she is not at Court.'

Richard Ashton snorted and nodded towards Catherine. 'She was once resident at the Brandon house, when it was the biggest whorehouse north of the river. Catherine, Duchess of Suffolk, as she now is, was once an innocent nine-year-old heiress whose wardship was sold by King Henry to that libertine Suffolk at a time when Henry was in debt to his armourer. By the time she was fourteen, she had been bedded by the old goat and the price of her silence and ongoing acquiescence to what was occurring between the sheets was the title that she now proudly wears like a battle wound.'

'Charles was once your friend,' Kate reminded him, 'and thanks to him you remained safe with me when Norfolk was seeking to silence you.'

'I am well reminded of that,' Richard replied testily, 'but that doesn't mean that I'm prepared to expose my daughter to all the debauchery of the Court and those who hang around it.'

'You surely make too much of the risk,' Kate argued. 'As I understand it, our daughter Grace is merely being invited to reside in the Suffolk household in order to be a companion to Jane and as a sort of chaperone for her. Does it not work in the reverse direction? If Grace is to be a guardian of Jane's virtue, will Jane not likewise preserve Grace from any evil that might cross her path?'

'You are forgetting that there will be times when, according to Suffolk's scheming, Jane will be in the Prince's company at Hampton Court Palace, or wherever else he may be accommodated. Who then will be guarding Grace?'

Any further conversation on the subject was silenced when a nervous page clapped his hands for attention and announced,

'The Lady Jane will now graciously demonstrate to us the depth of her learning in the languages of the classical scholars.'

Jane, after a reassuring squeeze of the hand from Grace, rose from her place at the table, armed with a freshly printed and bound folio of the works of Plato and walked unsteadily to the head table, to stand in front of another of their guests, the scholar Roger Ascham, who had recently been responsible for instilling classical learning inside the somewhat defiant head of the young Lady Elizabeth.

Aschem nodded encouragingly as Jane piped her way through the passage she had learned rote-fashion, then drew to a tentative halt and curtsied graciously as the spattering applause spread round the Hall, led by her father.

'Well?' Catherine Suffolk enquired anxiously of Ascham.

Aschem smiled indulgently. 'She is well learned, for a girl of her age. More advanced than the Lady Elizabeth, despite the difference in their ages, but not so far advanced, I conclude, as our young Duke of Cornwall.'

'But can she learn alongside him?' Catherine persisted.

Ascham inclined his head. 'That will depend upon King Henry, will it not? In terms of scholarship, perhaps, but would I be correct in surmising that you are not so much concerned regarding your granddaughter's development as a scholar as you are regarding a developing relationship with the royal heir?'

'None of your damned business,' Catherine hissed back, before turning to return to her seat. 'Stick to your Greek and allow me to provide for Lady Jane's future role at Court.'

IV

'May I introduce my granddaughter, Lady Jane Grey?' Catherine Suffolk proudly asked as she ushered a slightly trembling Jane into the centre of the room.

Jane executed a wobbly curtsey to the fine ladies seated in a semi-circle, not knowing who was who, and thoroughly overawed by the occasion.

They were assembled in the main room of Edward Seymour's quarters on the ground floor of the 'Placentia Palace' of Greenwich. He had occupied these rooms ever since his sister Jane had first caught King Henry's eye, and he and his wife Anne had chosen to make them their main residence when in London, although Anne and the growing brood of children found their Sussex estate more comfortable.

Even though the main room was one of the most spacious on the ground floor, it was still in danger of feeling overcrowded, given the company that had assembled in order to watch the final, un-costumed, rehearsal for the masque to be performed at the May Day Banquet that was to be held upriver at Hampton the following week.

Thomas Seymour was to be the master of ceremonies, as well as acting the part of 'Pan, the God of the Wilderness', with the recently widowed Catherine Parr as 'The Queen of the May', following their success at the Christmas festivities.

The rehearsal came temporarily to an end and Edward Seymour, as host, effected the introductions for the benefit of Jane.

'Seated slightly back from the others, and next to the window, is the Lady Mary,' he told her, 'and this is her Senior

Lady, Mistress Catherine Parr. On the other end of the line of chairs is the Lady Elizabeth, who will be part of the masque when it is finally performed. My wife Anne you have of course met, but you may not have met my brother Thomas. When I was lately at Bradgate you had a little friend from whom you seemed inseparable — has she accompanied you to London?'

'Yes, my Lord,' Jane replied in a wavering polite tone, 'but she is presently back at the house of my grandparents. Where is Prince Edward?'

Her forthright question caused a slight ripple of mirth among the ladies and in order to spare her further blushes Lady Mary smiled at Catherine Suffolk and paid her a fitting compliment. 'You are to be congratulated on having preserved your youthful looks while having become the grandmother of such a beautiful child, my Lady Suffolk.'

Catherine smiled graciously, not sure whether or not it was a barbed reference to her child status when first bedded by Charles Brandon. 'She is, of course, not my natural grandchild, since she is the offspring of my husband's daughter by his first marriage, to the Princess Mary. Her mother, Lady Grey, is thereby a niece of His Majesty and this delightful granddaughter of mine by marriage is a cousin in some degree to the young Prince Edward, with whom she desires to share the advantages of a fine education.'

The chamber door opened and a liveried attendant, slightly out of breath, announced, 'His Majesty King Henry and the Duke of Cornwall.'

All the adults who had been standing dropped smartly to their knees, while the Ladies Mary and Elizabeth clapped their hands in delight. Unsure what to do, Jane curtsied and remained standing.

Henry smiled down at her from his impressive height. 'What a delightful child! Are you perhaps the Lady Jane of whom I have heard so much? The daughter of my niece, Frances Grey?'

'Yes, Your Majesty,' Jane croaked as she curtsied once again and kept her eyes demurely on the floor.

Henry turned to Prince Edward with a smile. 'See the beauty of the companion you may have in your schoolroom, should you choose?'

'Not if she's cleverer than me,' Edward pouted, and everyone laughed politely.

Henry smiled around the faces of the company and his eyes finally came to rest on Catherine Parr. 'Mistress Parr, is there some reason why your hand is glued to that of my long-serving ambassador to Germany, who only returns to my service when his credit has run out with the alehouse keepers of Vienna?'

Catherine let go of Thomas Seymour's hand as if it had suddenly become red hot and she blushed as Thomas offered an explanation.

'We were rehearsing for the May Day masque, Your Majesty.'

'Indeed?' Henry asked in a tone of disbelief. 'Well then, let us see how this mummery progresses. Pray give me an early sample of your proposed fare.'

As Catherine and Thomas began the opening dialogue, in which Pan met the Queen of the May in a sylvan grove named 'Windsor Forest', Henry sidled up to Edward Seymour and spoke quietly from the corner of his mouth.

'How go our relations with the Scots?'

'I fear that the Catholic faction will prevail, Your Majesty, and that the young Mary will be wedded to France.'

'All the more reason why we need good friends in Germany and the Low Countries ere we venture across the Channel to tweak Francis's nose. See to it that we send an ambassador without delay. And make it your dissolute brother Thomas — the less he holds the hand of the Lady Catherine, the better.'

Jane was destined never to share a school room with the young Prince Edward, principally because he was apprehensive that she might prove to be cleverer than him, and being bested by a girl was not something to be tolerated by a somewhat spoiled and over-indulged boy who was constantly being reminded that one day he would be King of England. But this did not prevent him seeking Jane's company on the many occasions when suitable young people of his age were invited to visit him in his own apartments at Greenwich, where he held court as if he were already the King and where he had his own troupe of minstrels.

On such occasions, Jane and Edward would chat happily regarding the things they were being taught by their respective tutors. Edward's interests, like his father's, were wide ranging and liberal in nature, from European and classical languages to religious philosophy, mathematics and the rudiments of music. Jane was also receiving a broad Renaissance education under private tutors such as John Aylmer and Michelangelo Florio in the house of her Suffolk grandparents, and even though their original ambition for Jane to be educated daily with the heir apparent had not come to fruition, Jane pleaded with them to resist her own parents' insistence that she be returned home, where the education had been more rigid and the discipline more stern.

But if Jane was happy and content in her new environment, Grace Ashton would have preferred to go home to the familiar fields and hedgerows of her family estate in Leicestershire. She was not invited to Court and in fact, she rarely saw outside the

Suffolk family's London residence, an overcrowded mansion in Borough High Street, across the Thames in Southwark, where the only young people remotely of her age were young serving boys and girls. Having nothing in common with them and being strictly reminded, on an almost daily basis, that she was 'a different class of girl altogether', she was housed in a single room immediately beneath the tiled roof and tended to hang morosely around the kitchen, where the cook would find her tasks to occupy her attention, if only to prevent her getting under everyone else's feet.

She had written several times, in her childish scrawl, to her parents, begging to be brought home, but her pleas had come to nought. Although concerned for her happiness, Richard and Kate Ashton were constantly reassured by their influential neighbour Henry Grey that Grace was being well cared for and that the Greys continued to deem it a great favour for their daughter Jane to have a companion and chaperone on those days when she was not learning all about life at Court.

Even when Jane was not at Court, she was being treated more like the daughter of the house, whereas Grace ate with the servants and lived a solitary existence in the room under the eaves of the tall three-storied town house. Jane had not forgotten Grace, but somehow their paths crossed less often as the weeks passed.

V

As the summer of 1543 commenced, Catherine Parr had more to think about than dressing Lady Mary's hair and laying out her gowns. At the May Day Ball, King Henry had made a great point of complimenting her on her portrayal of the May Queen and had insisted on partnering her in some of the slower dances that followed, during which he offered to write other masques in which her 'fair beauty' might be shown to best effect, while reminding her that Thomas Seymour, to whom she seemed to have become attached, would shortly be leaving England on a perilous mission to the Low Countries from which he might never return.

Lady Mary looked upon the growing number of occasions when she was invited to events at Court as further confirmation of the extent of her long awaited reconciliation with her father, little knowing that his real motivation was that she never failed to bring Lady Catherine Parr with her. It was her still youthful attendant who was the real object of Henry's attention and even when he sought out Catherine more and more for conversations in quiet corners, it never occurred to the somewhat straight-laced Lady Mary that this was other than her father's implied acknowledgment of his daughter's wise choice of a lady-in-waiting.

She learned the true state of things at the same moment as the other members of Court, who were assembled by summons in late June to be advised that Lady Catherine Parr had graciously accepted the role of Henry's sixth Queen of England and that the marriage was to be celebrated in only two weeks' time at Hampton.

City merchants celebrated the rapid torrent of orders for new tunics, hose, gowns, jewels, horses, livery and linen as Courtiers adjusted quickly to the news and prepared themselves to parade in all their finery both at the simple service conducted by Archbishop Cranmer inside the chapel at Hampton on 12th July and the Wedding Banquet that followed.

Meanwhile, the Scottish Parliament had finally repudiated any possibility that their young Princess Mary would become betrothed to Edward of England, and they nailed their colours even more firmly to the mast by cementing the 'Auld Alliance' with France by way of a marriage proposal between their princess and the young Dauphin.

Catherine Parr soon began a campaign for the reinstatement of the royal daughters she had come to know so well and most notably the Lady Mary, whom she had served as an attendant Lady. Basking in the warm glow of a new marriage, this time with a demure and almost matronly consort who seemed to attract no scandal and who was happy to nurse her new husband as she had once nursed her previous one, Henry was easily persuaded that the ultimate succession ought to be formalised, in the event that anything should happen to his son.

It was a delicate matter and it was essential that Parliament approve what was being proposed, if it was to be effective in preventing any disputes after Henry's death. Catherine's main concern was to restore Lady Mary to her rightful place in the line of succession, despite her strident and unapologetic adherence to the 'old' Catholic faith. But this could not, in all logic or conscience, be achieved without granting the same rehabilitation to the more liberally Protestant Elizabeth, and so the resulting Act of Succession returned both Mary and

Elizabeth to the line of succession, behind Edward, any potential children of his, and any potential children of Henry by Queen Catherine. But, as if to preserve something of his previous rejection of two former wives, Henry insisted that his two natural daughters retain their illegitimate status.

There was little apprehension that the Act would ever need to be implemented, given that Edward was a robust child approaching seven years of age, who could be expected to grow into manhood, then take his pick of the available princesses of Europe. But, conscious of his own mortality and about to embark for France at the head of a large army of invasion whose ultimate target was Paris, Henry decided to reinforce what Parliament had just enacted in a will.

He dictated it to Archbishop Cranmer, in which he confirmed the succession that was now statutory, but added that should this for any reason fail then the line of succession should continue through the ultimate heirs of his deceased younger sister Mary, but excluding Frances Grey. This made her daughter, Lady Jane Grey, the ultimate in line to the throne, should Edward, Mary and Elizabeth all be childless and dead when the will came to be implemented.

Few were aware of the terms of this will and life at Court continued under the more gentle influence of the new Queen, who basked in the gratitude of the two royal daughters who had been restored to the inheritance. They could not have been more different in nature and outlook, with the more sombre Mary, now obliged to pay due respect to a former lady-in-waiting who had become her stepmother, somewhat set apart from the rest of those who gathered regularly to amuse young Prince Edward.

Grace Ashton, meanwhile, was back where she belonged, on her father's estate at Knighton and eagerly anticipating her forthcoming seventh birthday, on which she had been promised her own pony. Since Jane Grey was still at Court, their shared nurse Mary Calthorpe, when not in attendance on the young Lady Catherine at Bradgate, was able to devote more attention to the high-spirited young 'Mistress' at Knighton.

'Lord preserve us, young lady!' Mary exclaimed as she examined the room that Grace had allegedly tidied. 'What did they teach you in that fine house in London? Or were you waited on hand and foot, as you expect to be upon your return here?'

'They taught me nothing, Nanny, other than the life of a servant. I was not waited on — rather I was expected to wait on them. Even Jane, who was treated by the Brandons as if she was their daughter, while I was nothing but a kitchen girl. I did, however, learn how to roast meat on a fire.'

Mary's heart softened as she saw the memory of betrayal written across the poor lass's crestfallen face and she laid a comforting hand on Grace's shoulder. 'More fool them, then, that they couldn't see what a real lady was in their midst.'

'I don't suppose I'll ever see Jane again,' Grace said wistfully. 'She'll be married off to some fine lord and will probably have a big house in the country, or perhaps a mansion in London like the one where I worked in the kitchen.'

'Do you miss Jane?' Mary asked.

Grace nodded, almost in tears. 'She was my only friend, for as long as I can remember. But she forgot all about me when she was always going to Court and playing with the Prince.'

'I miss her too,' Mary admitted, choking back a tear. 'Lord knows that the pair of you used to run me ragged when you were together, but I'd happily put up with that to see her back here with you, and the two of you covered in muck.'

Mary Calthorpe was not the only one feeling the absence of Jane. Although there was another Grey daughter, Catherine, aged four, both Henry Grey and his wife Frances missed having the lively Jane around the place, always up to mischief with her young friend Grace, and they were fearful for her fate, alone in the wickedness that they had both experienced at the court of King Henry.

They trusted her grandparents, the Duke and Duchess of Suffolk, to treat her kindly and steer her out of the way of any obvious harm, but Jane would soon be of an age to attract young men, and their many earlier ventures to Court had left them with no illusions about the opportunities that existed in London for seduction and betrayal. Jane had always been stubborn and headstrong and they feared for her future should she be preyed upon by some randy young gallant in search of an heiress, or simply an outlet for his lust.

Richard Ashton's insistence that Grace be sent back to Knighton had led to a certain cooling of relations between the Greys and the Ashtons. Henry Grey complained that Jane had been left without her companion and chaperone, to which Richard Ashton had retorted, with some heat, that she had never been either, since Jane had effectively abandoned Grace in order to pursue a life of sorts at Court, and Grace had never been treated by those in the Suffolk household as other than an extra house servant. When Grey had announced that if any harm befell Jane, he would hold Ashton responsible, Ashton retorted that the remedy lay in their own hands. They could bring Jane back home, as he had done with Grace, but if they preferred to hazard her welfare in the hope of seeing her advanced in royal circles, then the responsibility rested with them.

VI

Two years passed, during which Charles Brandon, Duke of Suffolk, died. His widow became closer to Queen Catherine, and two rumours began to circulate in Court. The first was that Queen Catherine was using her position to drive through dangerous reforms in religious practice that would cause a rebellion, and that Henry was too old and weak to resist. When Henry confronted her with this accusation, she managed to persuade him that her recent arguments with him regarding further Reformist measures had been intended only to take his mind off the suffering caused by his ulcerous leg.

The other rumour was that Henry had fallen for the alluring 'Madame Suffolk' and was seriously contemplating removing Queen Catherine from the throne, given her failure thus far to bear him any children and replacing her with Charles Brandon's widow. Catherine lost no time in assuring the Queen that there was no truth in the rumour and given the warm friendship that had developed between them, she was believed. However, the two ladies agreed that it might be better were the Suffolk widow to withdraw to the family estate she had inherited some years ago in Lincolnshire.

This was the imposing Grimsthorpe Castle and within weeks of suppressing the alleged scandal involving her and the King, the Dowager Duchess of Suffolk had moved her entire retinue north. Along with her, as an unspoken adopted daughter, she took Jane Grey, who rapidly tired of being even an honoured member of the new household, given that opportunities no longer existed to visit Court, or idle away her hours with Prince Edward.

Grimsthorpe was little more than a two day ride away from Jane's own family home at Bradgate and she had little difficulty in persuading her parents to collect her in the family coach and bring her back to the familiar scenes of her earlier childhood and memories that were now nearly two years old.

As Jane stepped down from the coach on her father's supporting arm, her eye fell on a subdued looking Grace Ashton, standing to the side of their old Nanny Calthorpe. She gave a cry of recognition, slipped from her father's grasp and ran towards Grace with widespread arms. Then, a few feet short, she stopped dead in her tracks when Grace showed no sign of opening her arms for an embrace and instead stood staring at her accusingly.

'Grace!' Jane said. 'Do you not recognise me? Have I grown up so much that you don't know who I am?'

'Why should I?' Grace replied sullenly. 'In London I barely saw you, but was left to join the other servants. You didn't want to know me when you played with Prince Edward and now you want me to be your friend again?'

A tear formed in Jane's eye as she dropped her arms to her side, lost for words.

Mary Calthorpe took Grace's arm and pulled her towards Jane. 'Well, there's a fine welcome home for the girl who used to lead you into such mischief! And as for you, Lady Jane, have you no hug for the Nanny who always managed to make you presentable when you rolled in all the muck with your friend? I don't know which of you was the worse — but I do remember that it was nigh impossible to keep you two apart.'

Jane raced over, threw her arms around Mary and began to sob. 'Court was fine enough, but it never felt like home. I can't wait to explore the grounds again!'

Grace reached out a hand and pulled Jane sideways so that they were sharing the hug with Mary Calthorpe. 'Does that include rolling down to the fishpond and counting the carp?'

'Yes, of course it does, dearest Grace! I can't tell you how much I've missed you, because you won't believe me.'

'I will, because I know how much I've missed you,' Grace croaked, and Mary Calthorpe was all but pushed to one side as the two young girls hugged each other joyfully and cried on each other's shoulders.

'Do you miss being at Court?' Grace asked Jane as they rambled slowly among the grazing fallow deer in the sprawling park that lay to the north of Bradgate House. Jane had been back home for almost a year now, and was now a little over nine years old.

'Of course,' Jane replied, 'although it all seems like an old dream these days. I miss all the fine food and the servants who would bring us whatever we asked for. But most of all I miss talking to Prince Edward. We became very good friends and he always singled me out when he wanted an honest opinion on something or other. He couldn't ask the Lady Mary, because she disapproves of almost every idea in his head and as for Lady Elizabeth, I'm afraid she's not very given to study and she would distract me by making me giggle with some silly jest or other. It's perhaps best that neither of them will become Queen, because Mary's too strict and Elizabeth's too sort of giddy-headed. Edward is just about right, I think. He reminds me of you.'

'How?' Grace asked, puzzled.

'Well, I got the feeling that he was always telling me the truth, the way you do. Whatever he said, he seemed to believe it to be true and he never hid the truth behind fancy words and gestures, like so many Courtiers do, or so I hear.'

It fell silent for a few moments, until Grace's concern got the better of her. 'Do you think you'll ever be obliged by your father to go back to the Brandon house?'

'I don't think that likely,' Jane replied. 'Certainly not the house in London, where we both lived. That was only ever needed when my grandparents were received at Court and now that my grandfather's dead, my grandmother prefers the castle at Grimsthorpe. And now that we're so far away from Court and she can't present me to Edward every week, like a dish of sweets, I'm no longer of any use to her.'

'Use in what way?' Grace asked.

Jane sighed. 'My grandmother hinted that I might one day be married to Prince Edward, if I make myself agreeable to him. I think that's why she kept taking me to see him, but that can't happen anymore, clearly, now that she's in Lincolnshire and I'm no longer important to her.'

'Just think!' Grace mused out loud. 'I might one day be the best friend of the Queen of England! I will still be your best friend if that happens, won't I?'

'Of course,' Jane reassured her. 'And then Nanny Calthorpe won't be able to order us about any more. I might order her about instead. "Pass me that cushion, Nanny Calthorpe", or "Please fill my wine goblet, Nanny Calthorpe." Wouldn't that be something to look forward to?'

At court Edward Seymour visited Prince Edward on his way to an audience with King Henry.

Prince Edward smiled as the entrance of Edward Seymour was announced. 'Welcome to my daily audience and what have you brought me?'

'Nothing, as you can see,' Edward Seymour replied, 'other than news of more suppression of the unruly Scots. How go your studies?'

'I look forward to the day when they go out of my life completely. As to how I progress in learning, you must needs ask my tutors, those boring old men who occupy most of my days. It grows tedious here without the company that I was wont to enjoy. Even my sister Mary, who hides away from me in her own house. As for Elizabeth, she does not visit as often as she did, now that Jane Grey has been withdrawn from Court by her demanding grandmother. When I am King, I shall order that there be no more learning in this land, merely endless games and cakes. And prayer of course, to preserve us all from the anti-Christ in Rome.'

'Is that what you are being taught?' Edward Seymour asked, concerned to hear such religious bigotry from the mouth of a nine-year-old. 'That the Pope is the anti-Christ?'

'So my tutors teach me,' the young prince nodded. 'In years past, the fear of God's damnation governed the lives of men through the mouths of priests who grew fat through their insistence that they alone held the keys to Heaven. Was it not so? Am I being taught falsehoods?'

'I am no scholar,' his uncle replied, 'but there are many in this kingdom that you will one day rule who believe otherwise — that salvation lies through the old way of worship.'

'Like the Lady Mary?' the prince countered. 'Spending half your days on your knees, while some fat old man mumbles Latin over your head? No wonder she is so miserable.'

'Nonetheless, it is what she believes,' Edward Seymour insisted. 'She was brought up by her mother — the late Queen Katherine — to worship God in the old way, just as you are being taught the Reformist beliefs. You must surely allow men to worship as they choose?'

'Enough of this boredom! You begin to sound like my tutors and I will not be told what to believe. Have you no business with my father?'

'Indeed I do, which is why I am here at Greenwich today.'

Edward looked hard at his uncle. 'You would seek to remain in my good favour?'

'An uncle should always look to his nephew's happiness,' Edward Seymour replied noncommittally.

The prince smiled. 'Quite so. What I wish from you is that you bring the Lady Jane back to Court.'

'Why so?'

'Because she amuses me and makes an otherwise dull day light up with her very presence. If she is here, my sister Elizabeth may also resume her visits, since they are good friends and they brighten the gloom that always seems to hang around my other sister Mary. Can you undertake to bring both Jane and Elizabeth back here at least once a week?'

'I can undertake to try, certainly,' Edward Seymour assured him as he contemplated in his mind how he might bring this about, 'but it is not for me to command your sister Elizabeth, who is a royal princess. However, if, as you say, the renewed presence of the Lady Jane will ensure the attendance of the Lady Elizabeth, then I can at least do my utmost to bring her back to London.'

'Is she not still here?'

'No, she has returned to her parents' estate in Leicestershire, but it is an easy three days' ride.'

After leaving his nephew, Edward Seymour lost no time in seeking admission to the King's Audience Chamber, where he found Henry in a depressed and reflective mood. Henry waved Edward into the chair beside him, called for wine and, as protocol demanded, was the first to speak.

'What news from Scotland?'

Edward Seymour sighed and shook his head. 'It is a nation in uproar, Your Majesty. Since the peace treaty following our victory at Solway Moss, Scotland has split further along religious lines. In some ways this has proved beneficial to our interests, since a group of Protestant rebels murdered that old misery Cardinal Beaton, whose voice was the strongest raised in favour of spiriting the Princess Mary across to France. But rumour has it that Francis himself is set to invade Scotland, in retribution for the murder of Beaton and in order to take Mary bodily across to France, perhaps as a prisoner, but certainly with a view to her betrothal to the Dauphin.'

Henry sighed and winced as he shifted his diseased leg onto a footstool. 'In truth, I did not summon you here in order to discuss Scotland. There are more pressing matters closer to home.'

'Your Majesty?'

'You have come from the Prince Edward?' When Seymour nodded, Henry further asked, 'And how did you find him?'

'With your leave, Majesty, I will speak freely. He grows petulant and is being indulged too far, in my loyal and respectful opinion. While I rejoice that he is being tutored in the Protestant philosophy, it is, I fear, being overdone and he is inclined to be intolerant of those with a more Romanist persuasion, most notably the Lady Mary. She still commands a following of her own, including Norfolk, Wriothesley and Gardiner, and I fear that unless the Prince is taught more tolerance ere he becomes King, our nation will experience as much uproar as the Scots, making us more vulnerable to

French invasion. Or possibly a Spanish incursion, given Lady Mary's ancestry.'

Henry nodded, head down deep in thought. 'And that is why I summoned you, Edward, since you are the person I can trust above all others. I feel in my bones that I am not long for this life and that Prince Edward will inherit my throne long ere he reaches manhood. This will involve a Regency and I would wish you, as the royal uncle, to lead that Council.'

'You would appoint me Protector by your will?'

'No, Edward, since such a high and singular honour bestowed upon one man alone might provoke resentment, most notably from your dissolute brother Thomas, the other royal uncle. Rather it shall be a Council of Regency, a gathering of the most worthy and talented nobles in the land, acting as my executors. They shall be given a wide power to govern by majority and in my will I shall make broad provision for them to award themselves as they see fit in order to dominate those who might seek to contest the succession. To you I entrust, but secretly, the duty of ensuring that Rome does not, by my death, regain its authority over the Church I have founded here in England.'

'You wish the Regency Council to promote the Protestant cause?'

'Yes, but not so openly as to cause rebellion among the stubborn Catholics who continue to resist reform. One of those is of course the Lady Mary and I do not wish Edward to be placed in a position in which he is obliged to commit her to the Tower.'

Edward Seymour's brain was racing with the possibilities that were opening before him. 'This might be more easily achieved were Your Majesty to begin a policy of removing, from their current positions of influence, those most likely to support the cause of Rome. By this means, when the time comes for Edward to take up the reins of kingship, they will be the more easily held down.'

Henry allowed himself a smile. 'You refer, of course, to Norfolk and his hangers-on? Your enmity with him reminds me most forcefully of the days in Council when he and Suffolk would almost come to blows. And before him, Cromwell and Wolsey. It seems there was never a time when Norfolk did not attract enemies.'

'All the more reason why he be removed from a position in which he can incite more, Your Majesty. If the devolution of power is to be made as smoothly as possible to a prince with a Protestant crusade to wage, then the less Romanists in Council the better.'

'Only Norfolk, say you?'

'Clearly Gardiner as well, Majesty, since he has ever sought to be Canterbury rather than Winchester. If Stephen Gardiner were to acquire the see of Canterbury, he would sell out to Rome by the end of the same week.'

'And Wriothesley?'

'I can manage him with one arm tied behind my back and there will need to be some continuity in legal quarters. So retain him as Chancellor, but leave him in no doubt that he will only exercise his drafting arm when it is jerked into life by a string attached to the Regency Council.'

Henry smiled. 'My instinct was correct, it seems. But there is one final matter. I wish the current Queen to receive a generous allowance on my death — let us say seven thousand pounds a year, paid directly from the Treasury — and to be afforded all due respect as Queen Dowager. She may also retain all her jewels, including those that came with her crown.

Can you see that this is honoured if I include it within the terms of my will?'

'Of course, Your Majesty, but let us not talk as if such provisions will be executed immediately.'

Henry looked sadly through the mullioned chamber windows, where a few hesitant and wispy flakes of snow were drifting down into the Palace gardens. 'The first snow of winter. I fear that I shall not live to see the first of the daffodils ere those snows recede.'

VII

Richard and Kate Ashton shook the snow from their riding capes and accepted the cups of mulled wine that they were handed by a server in the entrance hall to Bradgate House, while two grooms led their mounts to the warm straw of the adjoining stables. Henry Grey walked from the Great Hall with his hand extended in greeting.

'Richard — and Kate — thank you so much for making the perilous journey and in such dreadful weather. Come into the hall and warm yourselves by the fire.'

'So what is so urgent?' Richard Ashton asked as they stood in front of the cheerfully blazing logs, idly watching the pages erecting the trestles.

Henry Grey looked to his wife Frances for support as he answered. 'It concerns Jane, which of course means that it also concerns Grace, since Jane will not leave without her.'

'Leave for where?' Kate asked fearfully.

'We have another visitor, as you will discover in a moment,' Frances replied. 'Thomas Seymour, who now calls himself "Lord Warden of the Cinque Ports" in addition to "Master-General of the Ordnance". I assume that these were rewards from King Henry simply for being a royal uncle.'

Richard Ashton smiled as he recalled the wild and feckless youth he had first met at Wulfhall when he had arrived with Thomas Cromwell to escort his sister Jane back to London to be wooed into marriage by a much younger King Henry. 'He has done little else to earn such offices, as I understand it. But why is he here and why are we summoned?'

'And how does it concern Grace?' Kate demanded nervously.

Frances placed a consoling hand on her arm. 'Jane is summoned back to Court.'

'By the King?' Richard asked.

Henry shook his head. 'By the Prince Edward. It seems that he took a shine to our daughter when she was last at Court and Thomas Seymour has undertaken to escort her back there at Edward's request.'

'And Jane, as usual, will go nowhere without her constant companion,' Frances added.

Richard frowned. 'As Grace tells it, the last time they were down there, at the Suffolk house, she was hardly Jane's companion, but was treated like a lowly servant. We were obliged to bring her home and there was no indication that either girl missed the other. Jane only returned here after she grew tired of life at Grimsthorpe, and not because she was pining for Grace's company. Does your daughter wish to use ours as a mere travelling companion, only to abandon her once more to kitchen duties once they have arrived? And to where is it intended that she travel this time? Is Madam Suffolk back in London?'

Henry Grey looked across to the hall entrance and beckoned to the latest arrival with his free hand. 'Here is the man who can answer those questions. Thomas, I believe you remember Sir Richard Ashton?'

'Indeed.' Thomas Seymour smiled as the two men shook hands. 'He was ever by Cromwell's side, when not in the company of Lady Rochford, and was most instrumental in assuring my sister that it was safe to become Queen of England. How go matters with you, Richard?'

'Middling well,' Richard replied guardedly. 'Henry here advises us that Grace is once again to be called upon to chaperone Lady Jane, if only in theory. Before we consent to that, my wife and I wish to be reassured that she will be more respectfully accommodated as befits the daughter of a country squire, and not the spawn of a scullion.'

Thomas Seymour's face clouded. 'I have no knowledge of how she was treated when she lived in the Suffolk household, of course, but in mine, you may rest assured, she will be treated no differently from the Lady Jane herself.'

'And what does your household consist of?' Kate asked, suddenly much more alarmed.

Thomas Seymour smiled reassuringly. 'Think you that I would take two young girls into my house without adequate concern for their welfare? I am already seeking to employ a governess, since I remain as yet unmarried and therefore childless. It shall be her duty to guard the honour of the Lady Jane and her companion, who I have yet to meet, by the way. I am advised that your daughter remains at home today.'

'Indeed she does,' Richard confirmed, 'and she is destined to remain there until we have better assurance of what future lies in store for her back in London. It is obviously a matter for Sir Henry here whether or not Jane will be permitted to return to London, but until you give better account of the management of your household, she would be making that journey without my daughter in attendance.'

Back at Court, Edward Seymour had received news from the Senior Clerk of the office of the Earl Marshall of England that the Duke of Norfolk's son had been making use of the heraldic arms of Edward the Confessor, reserved solely for monarchs. This was the excuse Edward Seymour had been waiting for, and two days later, both father and son were in the Tower. Realising, too late, that his arrogance had led him to a point of no return, Norfolk made a full confession of having 'concealed high treason, in keeping secret the false acts of my son, Henry Earl of Surrey, in using the arms of St. Edward the Confessor, which pertain only to kings'. In desperation he surrendered all his estates to the King, but was advised that he was to be executed anyway. His neck was preserved only by the death of the ailing King Henry on the day before the sentence was to be carried out.

Henry had been dead barely a week, with his body interred, in accordance with his wishes, next to his beloved Jane Seymour in St George's Chapel in Windsor Castle, when the Regency Council met for the first time in the Council Chamber at Whitehall Palace. With Norfolk in the Tower, tremblingly expecting to receive a date for his execution with every entry into his cell and Gardiner excluded from the list of those chosen by the late King Henry to see his nine-year-old orphaned son safely through to his majority, the Council began, at Edward Seymour's insistence, by electing a leader. No-one was surprised when that leader turned out to be Edward Seymour himself, now calling himself the Duke of Somerset and 'Lord Protector of the Realm'.

The coronation of the new King Edward VI took place at Westminster Abbey a month after his father's death, at the hand of the Archbishop of Canterbury Thomas Cranmer, who publicly urged the new King to continue with the Reformist policies of the Church of England begun by his father and to see 'the tyranny of the Bishops of Rome banished from your subjects.' Lady Mary sat sourly through the proceedings before making great show of taking up residence in Hunsdon, in

Hertfordshire, an estate she had inherited in her father's will and which she set about extending into something only slightly less than a royal palace. Lady Elizabeth remained for a day or two longer, then retreated back to her childhood home at Hatfield, now happily free of the cramping influence of her pious older sister.

Edward Seymour's assumption of de facto power was complete once he persuaded King Edward to grant him letters patent that empowered him to appoint members of the Council in accordance with his own preference and consult with them only when it suited him.

Edward Seymour was now King in all but name.

VIII

'What's this?' King Edward demanded petulantly as Thomas Seymour bowed into the presence, followed by two puffing and sweating servants carrying between them a large object covered by a cloth. The object was placed on the ground and the servants withdrew as Thomas triumphantly whisked the cloth away, to reveal a toy fort made from wood and hand-painted to look like a grand castle.

'And what am I supposed to do with that?' Edward asked grumpily. 'I cannot eat it, I cannot spend it and it will not assist in my studies, so pray what is it for?'

'There is more, Your Majesty,' Thomas replied with an ingratiating smile. He reached inside the castle keep and withdrew two boxes, each of which contained a set of toy soldiers. 'See, I have provided you with two armies. The red army is besieging the castle, which is being defended by the blue army, and you may arrange them in any way you wish. It has all been made, on my commission, by one of the finest toy makers in London.'

'Uncle Thomas,' Edward reminded him haughtily, 'I am nine years old, I am the King of England and I have outgrown children's toys. At least when my Uncle Edward visits me, it is to tell me that my real army has further subdued the heretical Scots. When you can advise me that you have captured the Pope and await my instruction to have him executed in full public view on Tower Hill, then you may return and amuse me. In the meantime, don't — unless, of course, you wish to make me laugh with yet another of your pathetic excuses for not bringing back the Lady Jane.'

'I have not spared any effort in that regard, Your Majesty, but her parents — your own cousins the Greys — will not let her return to Court unless I can accommodate her in a family home, with a wife and children of my own. As you are aware, I am as yet unmarried.'

'But there must be others of your acquaintance with whom she may reside?' Edward argued. 'And here comes just such a likely prospect.'

The chamber doors had been opened by a liveried usher and the Dowager Queen Catherine stood hesitantly in the doorway as her arrival was announced. She caught sight of Thomas and blushed. 'Forgive me, I was not advised that Sir Thomas was attending upon Your Royal Highness.'

'He will be leaving shortly, if he knows what's good for him,' Edward pouted, 'and I will then be glad of your more amusing company, my good mother. How fare you?'

'In truth, dearest Edward, I am sorely vexed, by this man's sister-in-law, no less.'

'Anne Seymour?' Thomas asked, intrigued.

Catherine's face set in a sullen frown. 'Since your brother Edward became Protector of England, she behaves as if she were its Queen. She has grown so haughty of late and it is all she can do to receive me when I attend upon her. Now she has taken this foolish notion into her head that the jewels I wore when Queen are no longer mine to wear, even though it was expressed in the will of my dear late husband that I should inherit them as my own. She claims that as wife of the Lord Protector, she is nearer to being England's Queen than I am.'

'I care not which of you wears the baubles,' Edward replied languidly, 'but if you desire my intervention in the matter, Mother dear, there is something you can do for me in return.'

'I would gladly satisfy any wish of yours.' Catherine smiled unctuously back at her stepson.

'You have a house in London?'

'Indeed I do, at Chelsea Manor, which was graciously bequeathed to me in the will of your late father.'

'And what manner of household do you maintain?'

'One suitable to my station. I have a steward, a chamberlain, a cook and various attendants and kitchen menials. I also play host to the Lady Elizabeth and her governess, Katherine Champernowne, on those occasions when your dear sister attends upon you here at Court.'

'But the Lady Elizabeth is mainly at her house in Hatfield, is she not?' Edward queried.

Catherine nodded. 'Indeed that is so, but when in London she resides with me at Chelsea, along with her governess.'

'So if you were to add one more lady of high birth to your household, there would be a governess there to guard her virtue also?'

'Indeed, if the Lady Elizabeth were there. If not, I could always employ another governess, since your late father was more than generous in the annual allowance he bequeathed me.'

'So, then, your paths are clearly defined for you both,' Edward replied. 'Thomas here will have the Lady Jane brought back to London, once he has assured her parents that there is a governess installed in your Chelsea house, where she will reside when attending Court. It shall be your task, dear Mother, either to secure the services of a governess for the Lady Jane, or to invite the Lady Elizabeth to be companion to Jane Grey, sharing this Mistress Champernowne as their governess. In return I will enquire of Uncle Edward regarding the ownership of your former jewels. We are agreed?'

When Catherine and Thomas agreed, Edward lost no time dismissing them and they found themselves outside in the hallway, where Thomas turned a beaming smile on Catherine, reached out for her hand and kissed it.

'It seems we are destined to be involved in another joint enterprise, madam. I for one give thanks to God that we shall be able to collaborate on something so obviously close to the King's heart. This time it will not be a masque for the royal entertainment, but — unless I misjudge the matter — the reuniting of two persons whose inner urgings draw them close together. It may be that we shall be easing the journey of the future Queen of England.'

'What, Jane Grey?' Catherine asked, taken slightly aback by Thomas's forthrightness.

'And why not? She is of royal bloodline, she is comely, she is Edward's age and she pleases him. If we are of assistance in bringing them together, will they not be forever grateful, just as I was grateful to the Lady Mary for bringing us together some years ago now? As I previously alluded, it is a wonderful privilege to be the means by which two people may give effect to their inner urgings.'

'You speak of you and I, my Lord?' Catherine asked, slightly breathless and pink of countenance.

'No, my dear lady, I can speak only for myself. But we have business in Chelsea, do we not? Both new business and — perhaps — business of an unfinished nature.'

'The new business?'

'To establish a household sufficient to satisfy the Greys of Bradgate that it is suitable for their precious daughter. You must first either acquire a governess for the young lady, or persuade the Lady Elizabeth to return with hers.'

'And the unfinished business?'

'Perhaps that were best discussed when we reach Chelsea. I take it that I am invited thither?'

Three hours later, Catherine lay back on the bolster in her bedchamber, totally exhausted but glowing with satisfaction. Thomas Seymour slipped from her side and gazed down lustily at her sweating nakedness.

'Would you consent to regularising what we have just consummated?' Thomas asked.

'You wish to wed me?' Catherine replied.

'No, madam, I wish to bed you. And nightly, what is more. But if we are to establish a seemly household for the Lady Elizabeth and the guardian of her maidenhead, in order to attract the Lady Jane back to London and thereby fulfil King Edward's wish, we must legalise our romps between the sheets. Unless, of course, it pleased you not?'

'Believe me, Thomas, it pleased me. But I am but two months a widow and a former Queen, what is more. What would be the likely outcry, were we to marry so soon?'

'Outcry from whom? Clearly, since you are a widow and I a bachelor, there was naught of adultery about it. And who would be likely to deny either of us our happiness?'

'Your brother Edward, for one, under the influence of his sow of a wife, who likes me not, for reasons that I cannot fathom. The Lady Mary for another, since she has no experience of the torments of the flesh — or at least, it must be presumed not, since she shows no inclination towards marriage despite having passed her thirtieth year. And there is King Edward.'

'What should he care?'

'If we were to marry, his stepmother would become his aunt. He is not yet of a mature enough age to appreciate the need of men and women to be bound together under God's holy ordinance. And we would need his consent.'

'Surely, if by granting his consent he is making the perfect nest in which to rear the Lady Jane as his companion — and perhaps even his Queen in due course — then he would not withhold it? If we have the King's consent, who can gainsay us?'

'I will willingly become your wife, should Edward grant his permission.'

IX

'Do you bring me news that the Lady Jane is back in London?' King Edward demanded as he looked up from his Latin primer and waved his tutor out of the presence.

Thomas Seymour shook his head in feigned sadness. 'Sadly, that has not yet proved possible, Your Majesty. The Lady Elizabeth is reluctant to move herself and her governess from Hatfield House until the household at Chelsea is larger.'

'What does the size of it matter, if there be sufficient servants and a governess?' Edward asked testily.

'It concerns the presence or absence of a gentleman of the household, Majesty. While there are manservants enough to ensure the safety of the house against incursion, a lady living alone as the head of a household containing young girls is always at risk of being accused of running a ... well, that is to say...'

'A whorehouse?' Edward chortled. 'You cannot be serious, Uncle? My mother was left sufficiently provided for not to require the wealth from such an arrangement and she herself is hardly likely to attract any man with his eyesight intact. So what would induce her to allow the place to be run as a brothel?'

'It has been known, Your Majesty, as may be recalled from the unfortunate example of the establishment of the late Dowager Duchess of Norfolk. This was while you were still in swaddling, attended by your wet nurse, but it was in that household that the late Queen Catherine Howard fell from virtue with a variety of Courtiers, including several of her tutors and her Secretary Thomas Culpepper. It was not discovered until after she had become Queen and it led her to the Tower. The only blame that could be laid at the door of the Duchess herself was that, in the absence of any husband, she had grown lax in the supervision of her noble charges.'

'So my mother requires a husband, say you?'

'Yes, Majesty, that would be best.'

'Best for whom, Uncle? For my father's widow to remarry so soon would be an insult to my father's memory, would it not and cast doubt on the depth of her love for him while he was alive? Could it not be claimed that any man she now married had gained her affections before my father died, thereby suggesting that she was not satisfied with my father?'

'I am amazed by Your Majesty's grasp of such subtleties in affairs of the heart,' was all that a stunned Thomas could offer by way of reply.

'Do not underestimate my subtle mind in other matters either, Uncle,' Edward smirked. 'There is a Council meeting this morning, which no doubt explains your presence in Whitehall. I am also here, thereby giving everyone in Council the impression that I intend to attend. But I do not, since these meetings bore me even more than my tutors. But in the belief that I will be there, men like yourself seek audience ahead of the meeting, hoping to draw my support for schemes they have in their hearts. What is it you seek, Uncle?'

'I seek nothing,' Thomas lied, 'but I had thought it only appropriate to advise you, ahead of the meeting, that I intend to raise with other members of Council my concern at the latest intelligence, to the effect that my brother Edward foreswore a perfect opportunity to capture the Princess Mary of Scotland and bring her back to England.'

'It may concern you, Uncle, but it does not concern me,' Edward replied airily. 'In fact, I rejoice in that knowledge. Why should I press for the forced imprisonment of a young girl whose only misfortune is to be born the daughter of a king, just as I was born the son of one? I am well placed to know how it feels to be raised and nurtured like a rose in a royal glasshouse, taught what to eat, to drink, to say — even to think! And for what purpose should she have been captured? To be brought down here like an animal trapped in the hunt, kept away from her own family and raised like a sacrificial lamb in order to marry an English prince whom she has never met, never will meet until she is of betrothal age and may well not like what she sees. As, indeed, I may not.'

Thomas was stunned into silence.

'Well?' Edward demanded.

'I ... I had not thought of it in those terms, Your Majesty.'

'That is because you are not me, with endless hours to think of such things. Now leave me with the boredom of my studies and do not come back until you are able to advise me that the Lady Jane has returned to London.'

'And the marriage of the Lady Catherine?'

'I have said all I intend to say for one morning on the subject of marriage,' Edward pouted. 'Now leave me.'

Knowing looks were being exchanged around the Council table, which slowly turned to smirks as Thomas Seymour persevered in his efforts to persuade his fellow members that his brother Edward had failed in his latest mission against the Scots.

'He suppressed them again, did he not?' Thomas Cranmer challenged him.

'Yes, but why did he not then proceed into Edinburgh and on to the royal Palace to secure the person of the Princess Mary?' Thomas Seymour demanded.

Everyone turned to John Dudley for an explanation, since it was well known that he had been part of the action.

'I did urge him to do so,' Dudley complained, 'but he seemed more content to discharge the men and come home. His reason was, or so he said, that he had a nation to govern.'

'He behaves more like a king every day,' Thomas Seymour observed with a sour smile. 'Can anyone doubt that?'

'If he delights in the power he wields,' Wriothesley countered, 'then why is he not here with us today?'

'Perhaps he perceives himself to be above even the King's Council,' Dudley suggested. 'Perhaps even above the King himself.'

'His wife certainly behaves as if she were Queen,' Thomas Seymour threw in. 'I learned only a short while ago that she has withheld the jewels formerly worn by the Queen Dowager when she was Queen, claiming that she has the greater right to wear them, now that Edward is the Lord Protector. We should guard against such over-weaning arrogance, less it turn into a rebellion against the throne.'

'Enough, my Lord Admiral,' Wriothesley warned Seymour, 'less over-weaning arrogance be deemed a family failing of the Seymours. Not to mention a rivalry between brothers that could split the nation in two. I have no cause to love your brother, but at present he is the one who keeps this nation intact, until King Edward be of age. We have more important matters to discuss and the morning advances.'

As the Council concluded their business and its members began to drift away, John Dudley sidled up to Thomas Seymour with a sympathetic smile.

'It would seem that I am the only other member of Council who shares your concern regarding your brother's growing arrogance, Thomas. Even on the battlefield, he behaves as if

England and its army were his to command personally, as our late King Henry did in France.'

'Why can no-one else see it?' Thomas muttered.

Dudley placed a comforting hand on his arm. 'For as long as we two can see it and warn the other Council members to be on guard against it, that should be sufficient. But has anyone warned King Edward that he has clasped a viper to his bosom?'

Thomas gave a hollow laugh. 'King Edward concerns himself only with matters close to his own interests. Or indeed, his own heart. Like the Lady Jane.'

'Jane Grey, Henry Grey's daughter?'

'The very same. The only matter on which King Edward will converse with me is when she is to return to Court. He is obsessed with her, it seems, and we can forget any question of a match with the Scottish Mary for as long as Lady Jane is in his company.'

'Think you that he sees her as a future Queen?'

'I would not dismiss such a thought, John. She is certainly of considerable importance to him, and he has charged me with the duty of bringing her back to Court. But without somewhere suitable for her to lodge, her parents resist any such suggestion. I have hopes that she may join the household of the Queen Dowager in Chelsea, once it is suitably provided with a governess and perhaps a new husband for the Lady Catherine herself.'

'It would seem that whoever has the keeping of the Lady Jane has the strings to the King's heart.'

X

'You must see how you have offended some very important people, including our nephew,' Edward Seymour argued sternly as his brother Thomas stared back at him defiantly.

'But how can our happiness be the cause of offence to others?' Catherine pleaded.

Anne Seymour snorted derisively. 'You are the Queen Dowager, the widow of the late King Henry and the stepmother of the current King. It behoves you to lead a less flamboyant life.'

'How can getting married be deemed "flamboyant"?' Catherine demanded. 'And if we are discussing flamboyance, how does it for the wife of the convenor of the King's Council — a mere servant of the King — to strut around in jewels that belong rightfully around the neck of a Queen?'

'Which you are no longer,' Anne observed cattily.

'And you will never be,' Catherine spat back, 'for all that your husband seeks to usurp all power into his own hands!'

'That's enough!' Edward yelled, then turned to Thomas with an angry snarl. 'Since this lady is seemingly now your wife, perhaps you might wish to control her tongue!'

'And you might wish to do the same with yours,' Thomas retorted angrily as he turned and held out his hand for Catherine to take. 'Come, my dear. We will take ourselves where our marriage is more of a cause for celebration.'

'You may have to travel a good distance,' Edward sneered.

Thomas stopped and turned in the doorway. 'An excellent suggestion, brother dear. And since, in your kingly condescension, you supplied us with the very place, you may visit us with an apology in Sudeley.'

As they scurried, red-faced, towards their carriage, Catherine clung to Thomas's arm and looked at him with concern. 'Was that merely in jest, or should we really make plans to visit Sudeley?'

'Why not?' Thomas said. 'Clearly we need to leave London until the dust settles and where better than a castle in Gloucestershire? I have only ever once visited it, but with our London household transferred down there, then swollen with locally acquired servants, will it not attract the Lady Elizabeth and after her the Lady Jane?'

The news of the wedding between Queen Dowager Catherine and the most eligible bachelor at Court, Thomas Seymour, rattled through Courtly circles like cannon fire from an armed merchantman. From there it spread out like an inkblot across the counties closest to London, until, after a week, it reached the Lady Mary in her Hertfordshire retreat of Hunsdon. She immediately called for pen and ink and fired off a bad-tempered vellum to her sister Elizabeth, who she suspected of being too friendly with the former Queen. In her sharply-worded missive, she strongly counselled Elizabeth against having any further association with 'Madam Seymour', as she tartly referred to her.

Less than a day's ride away in Hatfield House, Elizabeth grinned at the angrily penned expression of pious indignation and called for her governess Kat Champernowne.

As the headstrong fourteen-year-old royal Lady and her intimate but more mature governess giggled over the deep scores in the vellum that betrayed the anger in Mary's hand when penning what read like an imperious command, the governess expressed her reservation. 'For all that she is too straight-laced, Lillibet, you should perhaps heed her words.'

'Heed her words, certainly,' Elizabeth replied, as she tossed back her shoulder length golden-red hair defiantly, 'but obey them, certainly not. There would seem to be good sport to be had in Chelsea. Let us lose no time in seeking it out — have my bags packed for travel on the morrow.'

John Dudley bowed as he kissed Catherine Seymour's hand and smiled across at Thomas as they stood by the fire to welcome him into their Chelsea house. 'I hear that you have a new royal lodger, Thomas.'

'Indeed we do,' Thomas replied proudly, 'and she has brought her own more intimate household, necessitating that we move to the more spacious Sudeley Castle without too much delay.'

'Does that household include a governess?'

'Indeed it does — Mistress Champernowne.'

'Then you would seem to be well positioned to invite the Lady Jane to journey back to Court.'

'Indeed we are,' Thomas confirmed proudly. 'It lacks only the time to undertake the three day journey to Bradgate.'

'I have estates in Warwickshire, as you are of course aware,' Dudley said disingenuously, 'and from there the borders of Leicestershire are but a day's ride. I should deem it an honour to be allowed to carry a despatch from you to Sir Henry Grey, inviting the young lady to reside in your household. Should agreement be forthcoming without inordinate delay, I could also undertake to provide her with a suitable armed escort for the journey back to London.'

Thomas looked enquiringly at Catherine, who smiled and nodded. 'It would give us more time to get to know the Lady

Elizabeth and prevail upon Mistress Champernowne to accept responsibility for a second charge.'

Thomas turned back to Dudley with a broad smile. 'You are most accommodating and we accept your generous offer. Some wine ere you depart?'

An hour later, John Dudley clattered his horse out through the gates of the Chelsea house with a broad smile on his face. 'They are all correct in their assessment of you, Thomas Seymour,' he murmured. 'All ambition and charm, but no brains.'

'I'm not going without you,' Jane insisted as she grabbed hold of Grace's hand and clung to it, her face crumpling with impending tears.

'But surely your parents won't send you if you don't want to go?' Grace suggested by way of comfort.

Jane shook her head. 'These new people who arrived yesterday sound very important and they told Father that the King has requested that I return to London. You can't refuse a king, can you?'

'I don't know,' Grace replied with disarming frankness, 'since a king never asked me. But where will you stay this time? Is Lady Suffolk leaving her estate in Lincolnshire?'

'No idea,' Jane replied sulkily. 'No doubt we'll find out when we go in to dinner today. I've been told by Nanny Calthorpe to wear my best gown and be polite and "demure", as she called it.'

They approached the front door of Bradgate House and saw Mary Calthorpe standing waiting for them with an anxious look on her face.

'If my parents say I can't go with you, then I can't,' Grace told Jane. 'And unless I'm treated better than I was last time, I don't want to go. You ignored me last time, remember?'

'That was before,' Jane insisted. 'It'll be different this time, I promise.'

Mary Calthorpe smiled appreciatively. 'This must be the first time you two came back to the house looking almost clean and presentable. Now go and wash your hands, comb your hair and change into your best gowns. The guests are waiting for you and the dinner's being held back until you take your places. At the high table this time, I'm told.'

Both girls groaned as they headed for Jane's suite of rooms, where they would both be given their final grooming.

'Here they come at long last,' Henry Grey announced with a relieved smile as the two girls walked into the Great Hall accompanied by Mary Calthorpe, who diplomatically fell two paces behind them, then made her way to the most senior of the servants' tables.

'Which of them is Jane?' John Dudley enquired. 'They look very similar.'

'Jane's the one in the blue gown, with the red hair showing under her cap,' Henry Grey told him. 'The other girl is her friend Grace Ashton, from the neighbouring estate of Sir Richard Ashton. If Jane is to journey back to London, then she insists on her friend accompanying her. They've been constant companions since the day they could walk.'

'That shouldn't be a problem,' Dudley assured him. 'The Chelsea house is quite spacious and they have plans to move to Sudeley Castle, which is even more commodious. And Mistress Champernowne is already there as governess to the Lady Elizabeth and can no doubt add them to her list of duties.'

He rose from his seat and walked towards a nervous looking Jane with a bow and a broad smile, as he indicated a vacant seat next to a boy of thirteen, who rose, along with his slightly older companion, as the two girls were led towards them.

'Good day, Mistress Grey. I am Sir John Dudley, Earl of Warwick, and this young man is my son Guildford. You might wish to take the vacant seat next to his, while your companion may take the seat next to my squire, Master Bestwick.'

The two girls took the seats into which they had been directed and Jane looked sideways at the good-looking, dark-haired boy beside whom she was seated.

He turned to meet her gaze and smiled openly as he gestured towards the table with his dining knife. 'Do you wish me to carve you some goose, Mistress?'

Jane shook her head with a faint grimace. 'No, thank you — far too greasy for my palate. Perhaps some of that pie.'

'As you wish,' Guildford replied and set about penetrating its crust with his knife and scooping some of its contents onto Jane's silver dish with the spoon that lay on the salver. He chose pork for himself and it fell silent.

His companion on the other side was having slightly more success in drawing Grace into conversation.

'Do you reside here as Lady Jane's companion, Mistress?'

'Almost,' Grace replied. 'In truth, I live on my father's estate of Knighton, half a day's ride to the south of here.'

'And your father is?'

'Sir Richard Ashton.'

'So you are Mistress Ashton?'

'Grace,' she told him.

The conversation seemed destined to end there, but at that point a serving girl reached between them with a wine jug.

'Your fathers have instructed that on this special day you may have wine, Mistress, provided that it is half water.'

'Thank you, Meg,' Grace said, then eagerly took a mouthful, but all but spat it out and grimaced. 'Another of life's disappointments. I've waited almost ten years to taste wine and now I think I prefer small beer.'

'It's certainly a taste one has to get used to,' her companion smiled. 'I'm Allan, by the way.'

Further up the table, John Dudley was seated between Henry Grey and Richard Ashton, with their respective wives on either side so that they might listen eagerly to the conversation.

'According to Thomas Seymour,' Dudley was advising them, 'the King was most insistent. He seems to value Lady Jane highly as a companion in his somewhat isolated youth, in which his daily activities are regulated and timed almost as if he were a monk in holy orders.'

'Not too many of those left in existence,' Richard said. 'Is he being weaned off the old ways, in the manner of the new Church?'

'Most certainly,' Dudley replied, 'since his tutors are chosen personally by Cranmer and they are all Reformist. By all accounts our young King is more inclined towards the Lutheran ways than his father ever was.'

'Jane has been raised with a similar outlook,' Henry Grey told them, 'which is no doubt why King Edward prefers Jane's company to that stern-faced older sister of his, who clings to her mother's Catholic beliefs as if they were the breath of life.'

'Who are we to know?' Richard Ashton asked. 'There was a time when we looked to priests for guidance in the matter of the avoidance of Hellfire, but now it seems that we are destined to walk the perilous road without signposts.'

'Very poetic,' his wife observed tersely, 'but are we not here to satisfy ourselves as to the suitability of Grace's next abode in London?'

'You need have no fear in that regard,' Dudley assured them. 'Seymour has gone to great lengths to collect a household in which they may reside with perfect safety and honour. Even to the extent of marrying the Queen Dowager, Catherine. It has been a matter of some scandal in Courtly circles, but King Edward seems to have given the union his blessing and there are few left who point the finger of accusation. Except Edward Seymour, of course, and particularly his wife. She and Catherine were once close, but now it would seem that Anne Seymour — or "the Duchess of Somerset" as she now insists on being addressed — has taken ill to the fact that her former friend is now her sister-in-law. And this seems to have driven the brothers further apart.'

'What else can you advise us regarding the household?' Frances Grey persisted.

Dudley smiled as he leaned forward to look into her face. 'There is already the finest governess in the land installed at the Chelsea house, since the Lady Elizabeth is in residence. Elizabeth is a few years older than your two daughters, but as a result Mistress Champernowne has considerable experience in restraining the intemperance to which young ladies are subject. She did so under the stern scrutiny of the Lady Mary for some years and anyone who can pass that exacting test is fit to be governess to anyone, I suggest.'

'But if her primary concern is the Lady Elizabeth,' Kate observed, 'how then will she have the time to appropriately supervise our own two?'

Dudley smiled. 'Seymour has thought of that also and has engaged two other ladies who Mistress Champernowne may train.'

'Would Seymour consent to Mary Calthorpe accompanying them down to London?' Kate asked. 'Our only other child, Thomas, is now over five years of age and a boy has less need of a nanny than a girl. We could spare her, as no doubt could the Greys here, were Baron Seymour to engage her as governess for both Jane and Grace. She has carried out those duties beyond complaint for all the years during which they have been growing up together and she was once a nun. She is also my aunt and I would feel far happier knowing that she is with Grace, given her unfortunate experience on her last sojourn in London.'

'And I likewise, in respect of Jane,' Frances Grey added. 'Mary has been a very good influence on our daughter and both girls are only happy when they are together. For my part I would consent to Jane returning to London, but she refuses to go without Grace and she can be very stubborn. If both Grace and Mary Calthorpe are to accompany her, then I have no doubt that she will be content.'

'It shall be as you wish,' Dudley agreed, 'and you may leave it to me to satisfy Seymour on that score.'

XI

'It will stamp out all remaining heresy, say you?' King Edward demanded to know as Archbishop Thomas Cranmer sat by his side with sheaves of vellum on his lap.

'Most definitely, Your Majesty, and by attaching your name to it you will be leading the cleansing of the Church of the worst excesses of idolatry. It is to be innocently entitled "The Revised Book of Common Prayer" and it will of course be printed in our own English tongue. It lays down the observances that are to be followed and does away with some of the mummery that appeals only to the ignorant, the credulous and the superstitious, such as the raising of the bread and wine and the absurd notion that it somehow becomes the blood and body of Christ. For too long your people have been held in thrall by such witchcraft and yours will be the hand that saves their souls from Purgatory, should you agree to sign the complete folio in due course. As Supreme Head of our Church you give the lead to others.'

'And how will it be enforced?'

Cranmer smiled. 'All parish clergymen will be ordered to adopt the new form, on pain of dismissal from office. Those who preach publicly against it will be accounted heretics and burned.'

'And those in high Church office who oppose it?'

'Only Gardiner and Bonner are likely to do so, Your Majesty, and the Tower would seem to hold the means of silencing them.'

'What of my sister Mary?'

Cranmer was ready for this question, but waited for an appropriate few seconds before replying. 'Should she speak out against it publicly, then of course we could use that as the ground for disinheriting her from the succession once again, rather than have her condemned as a heretic. At worst, a period in the Tower for treasonously speaking out against Your Majesty's policies. But if I might make so bold, it might be better to allow her to worship in her own way in private, but threaten to take away that privilege should she prove troublesome.'

'Excellent!' Edward clapped his hands together in delight, but it was not so much in appreciation of Cranmer's wise counsel as the fact that the chamber doors had swung wide open, to admit Thomas Seymour and Lady Jane Grey. 'You may leave us and I will sign the document in due course,' Edward told Cranmer brusquely and the Archbishop bowed to one side, then slunk out of the Audience Chamber.

King Edward rose from his throne seat and walked part way down the carpet with his hands extended to grasp those of Jane Grey, as she attempted to curtsy, but he held her up by her elbows. 'No need for that nonsense among good friends such as ourselves. Uncle Thomas, you are now finally forgiven for your effrontery in marrying my stepmother without my leave. You kept this promise at least and, tell me, dearest Jane, does my uncle keep you in conditions appropriate to your station as a royal lady?'

'His house is certainly well appointed, Your Majesty — sorry, Edward — and it must indeed be suitable for even better than I, since the Lady Elizabeth is also in residence there.'

'And does that dreadful fusspot Mistress Champernowne also act as your governess? If so, I will give orders that she treat you more kindly than she does Elizabeth.'

'I have been allowed my own governess, thank you anyway, Edward. She has travelled with me from our estate of Bradgate and she has been my governess for as long as I can remember. I was also allowed to bring my childhood companion, Grace Ashton.'

'This is all excellent,' Edward beamed. 'Now, how much did you hear of what the Archbishop was boring on about as you entered?'

'I heard only something about allowing the Lady Mary to worship in her own preferred way.'

'And what think you? Should all people be so permitted?'

'Not if they thereby run the risk of falling into heretical sin, surely?'

'And how may such sin be avoided, say you?'

'By diligent reading of the Bible and communion with God in prayer.'

'An excellent response!' Edward enthused. 'It seems that our perceptions of the role that God plays in our lives are well aligned. You will assist me in drawing up further documents on the future that our Church should take?'

'I am no scholar, as you know,' Jane reminded him.

Edward simply smiled and led her by the hand to the chair next to his. 'Matters of scholarship we may leave to the Archbishop, but you and I may instruct him as true believers in the new religion and he may then convert our beliefs into procedure. Uncle Thomas, you may leave us, since we have much to discuss and you no doubt have many matters to attend to in the ordering of your household.'

For the next six months, life at the Chelsea house settled into a happy routine. Jane was accommodated in a suite of rooms on the second floor, with Mary Calthorpe in an adjacent room that was accessed by way of Jane's. Grace had her own room a few doors down from Jane's and between the two was a second suite of rooms, occupied by Lady Elizabeth, with her governess Kat Champernowne in the same sort of adjoining chamber to her mistress's bedchamber that Mary had in respect of Jane's.

All three girls — Elizabeth, now fourteen years old, Jane approaching eleven and Grace a few months behind Jane — were allocated places at the main table in the Hall of 'Chelsea Manor', as the house was known, and Grace was relieved that she was not being hidden away with the servants. Jane was in attendance on King Edward for several afternoons during the week, but the monotony, for Grace at least, was relieved by the fact that the two girls from Leicestershire were regularly attended upon by Guildford Dudley and his companion Allan Bestwick.

There was a long garden behind the house, planted with fruit trees and with a large flower bed in which a gardener maintained an impressive collection of roses, and on days when the weather permitted, the four young people would walk and talk.

For Jane and Guildford the conversation was mainly concerning matters that were occurring at Court; Jane was obviously able to supply Guildford with much detail regarding her regular conversations with King Edward, which Guildford would dutifully report back to his father the Earl of Warwick, as he had been instructed to do. From Jane, Guildford learned that the young King frequently expressed his frustration at being so closely confined within his suite of rooms and often declared his wish to be as free as other youngsters of his age. Jane had not the remotest idea that she was being used as a source of intimate information regarding the royal moods.

Grace and Allan, by contrast, could speak only of their own childhood memories and their hopes for the future. Since Grace was only just approaching her eleventh year, she had no realisation that the warm glow that she felt whenever she was in Allan's company was the prelude to something more deeply emotional; all that she knew was that the days seemed sunnier when he visited her and that they never seemed to run out of things to talk about.

After several such visits, Grace felt that she already knew the small village by the river, with its parish church and a few cottages clustered along its single street, one of which was home to Allan's family, who lived alongside the farrier's shop that provided the many Bestwick children with their livelihood. Allan, for his part, was intrigued by the glimpse that Grace gave him of life as the daughter of the lord of a modest rural manor, growing up alongside a childhood companion related to royalty.

The major event during that settling in period was the announcement, by a somewhat startled but overjoyed Catherine Seymour, that she was with child and due to give birth in September. Despite her three previous marriages, the most recent one to the King of England, Catherine had never conceived, and now, in her mid-thirties, she was about to experience something she had only ever witnessed in other women.

One night, Jane was having difficulty sleeping, an ailment she put down to the heavy supper that was still lying just below her breastbone. As she listened to the hoarse breathing and occasional snore of Mary Calthorpe through the open door of the adjoining chamber, she became aware of other noises, this time through the thin plaster wall behind her bed head.

The chambers next to hers were the ones occupied by Lady Elizabeth, with whom she had resumed the easy friendship that had developed during their earlier meetings with King Edward. Their paths did not cross too often these days and Elizabeth seemed to find her own amusements with attendant musicians and scholars, but they would meet at mealtimes and Jane looked up to the young woman almost four years her senior, taking fashion guidance from her and listening to her reminiscences of life at Hatfield House with her horses and country gallops.

What lay immediately behind the thin plaster at the head of Jane's bed was Elizabeth's bed chamber and Jane was therefore puzzled to hear giggles and a male voice raised in playful jest. Then she heard a slap and a squeal of laughter, followed by a woman's voice raised in admonition and a man's reply. This was followed by raised voices and the angry slamming of a chamber door.

Jane was still trying to decide what it all meant when there came a light tap on her chamber door and around the door from her adjoining main chamber came the pale face of Grace Ashton.

'May I come into your room?' Grace asked timidly. 'I'm a little frightened by all that disturbance.'

'What was it?' Jane asked.

Grace shook her head. 'All I know is that as I peered out of my chamber door I saw Baron Seymour storming down the hallway with a red face. I think he was angry about something.'

'More likely embarrassed,' came the stony voice of Maryy Calthorpe as she appeared from her own bedchamber, her hair tied in the ribbons that she wore for sleep. She looked at Grace disapprovingly. 'And you have no business walking the hallways in your nightgown, Mistress Ashton. Get back to your own room immediately.'

'But —' Grace began to argue, only to be silenced by Mary Calthorpe's raised hand.

'You have nothing to fear. The disgraceful proceedings are over for another evening. But if Mistress Champernowne does not report them, I will.'

XII

It was impossible not to notice the glum atmosphere in the Hall as Jane and Grace came in from a morning in the garden, walking and talking with Guildford and Allan. Lady Elizabeth rose hastily as they entered, leaving her dish of meat unfinished. Avoiding their gaze and ignoring Jane's enquiry as to what might be the matter, she all but ran from the hall, with Kat Champernowne fluttering closely behind her.

Grace asked a red-faced Mary Calthorpe why Elizabeth and her governess were making such an unseemly exit from the communal dinner table.

'They're both mightily embarrassed, Mistress, and with good reason, the pair of them. The Lady Elizabeth for encouraging it and Mistress Champernowne for allowing it.'

'What, Nanny?' Grace asked, frustrated with the answer and agog for any whiff of scandal in an otherwise boring household.

'The Lady Elizabeth has been asked to leave, and Mistress Champernowne is to accompany her to Sir Anthony Denny's house in Hertfordshire. Cheshunt, I believe.'

'But why?' Jane demanded, equally irritated by the reticence to give details.

Mary Calthorpe looked round briefly, satisfied herself that there were no servers currently in the Hall and lowered her voice to a whisper. 'The Master's been interrupted in Lady Elizabeth's bedchamber, where the pair of them were seen in an embrace of sorts — at least, that's what Lucy the laundress says. Mistress Kat's too embarrassed to discuss it with me, since she's clearly failed in her most important duty.'

'I saw the Master leaving Lady Elizabeth's bedchamber a few nights ago!' Grace chimed in excitedly. 'Was that the time when it happened?'

'One of them, seemingly,' Mary replied with a disapproving frown. 'Lady Catherine is said to be most put out and intends to move to Sudeley Castle for her lying in, living apart from the Master.'

'But she's not due until the autumn!' Grace pointed out. 'And what will happen to us?'

Mary frowned and knitted her brows in vexation as she explained, 'Well, you clearly can't remain here, if the Master engages in that sort of thing with young girls. So it's either Sudeley Castle with Lady Catherine, or back home.'

'But the King wants me in London!' Jane wailed.

Mary shrugged her shoulders. 'Be that as it may, I owe it to both of your fathers to preserve your good names, and clearly they would be lost were you to remain here, amidst all this ungodliness. There's nowhere else you can go, is there?'

'There might be, if you'd come with us,' Jane replied eagerly. She turned to Grace with big, wide, pleading eyes. 'Durham House? Do you think that Guildford could persuade his father to provide us all with accommodation?'

'I'm sure he could!' Grace replied encouragingly. 'And then I'd get to see Allan every day!'

'Who's this "Allan", and where have you been meeting him?' Mary asked suspiciously.

'Oh Nanny,' Grace laughed, 'don't be so stuffy! It's Master Bestwick, who calls several times a week. He was in the garden with us this morning. You should know — you were following us round the garden like one of the bloodhounds on the Bradgate estate.'

'I'm not so sure that I like the comparison,' Mary replied huffily, 'and I had no idea that you and he had got so close as to exchange first names so freely. I'd be inclined to instruct you to see less of him, except I know that the best way to get you to do something is to tell you not to.'

'It's nothing like that, honestly, Nanny. It's just that we're such good friends and he's so easy to get on with and —'

'I think I can work out the rest for myself, young lady, since I well remember how my niece turned into your mother in just such a fashion. But you're not yet even eleven years old and far too young to be taking a fancy to a young man.'

'He's sixteen,' Grace pointed out, 'and girls can get betrothed at twelve.'

'Don't you go getting ideas like that into your head, young lady.'

'What about Durham House?' Jane butted in, anxious for the conversation not to drift away from her need to continue attending Court.

'I suppose there's no harm in you asking,' Mary conceded, 'but you're not going anywhere near the place until I'm assured that there'll be room for me as well.'

It was not until three days later that Guildford and Allan once again presented themselves to the Steward of Chelsea Manor and were admitted to the house that Lady Elizabeth had left only the previous day in a coach loaded with her clothing and other bags.

Jane and Grace had carefully planned what each of them was to say and by agreement it was Grace who first broached the topic as she walked side by side with Allan Bestwick along the lawn.

'I hope that you and Guildford will make a special effort to visit us more frequently this week, since we must depart for our estates ere the end of the week.'

Allan stopped dead and turned with an apprehensive look. 'You can't mean that? Have you in some way annoyed the Lady Catherine? I know Jane can sometimes be a little headstrong and even mischievous, but surely not sufficient to deserve banishment from London? And what will King Edward say, if Jane can no longer visit him?'

'In truth, it's nothing we've done,' Grace told him with a crestfallen look. 'But Lady Catherine will be taking herself off to Sudeley for her lying in, leaving Baron Seymour here alone, and clearly it would not be seemly for two young ladies to remain, even if they have a chaperone of sorts between them.'

'Surely the Lady Elizabeth will also be remaining?'

'She's already left, and in some disgrace.'

'What sort of disgrace?'

'We're not supposed to know, but we've contrived to discover that it had something to do with Sir Thomas being discovered in her bedchamber.'

Allan's jaw dropped and he called loudly to Guildford. 'Guildford, has your father said aught to you regarding the Lady Elizabeth leaving here in disgrace?'

'Only that she has transferred to her house in Hertfordshire. I heard nothing regarding "disgrace". Do please tell! My father will be fascinated to hear of it.'

Breathlessly, the two girls recounted what little they knew of the matter, and Grace's contribution was clearly the more impressive, involving as it did the sight, by her, of Thomas Seymour being banished, dressed only in his nightshirt, from Lady Elizabeth's chambers.

'Would you be prepared to repeat all this to my father?' Guildford asked.

It was Jane who answered, after reaching out her hand to rest it on Grace's arm in a silent warning to let her pick up the conversation. 'We shall both require something from him in return,' she said quietly with lowered eyelids.

'How much?' Guildford enquired, reaching for the purse at his belt.

Jane shook her head. 'Not money, but something of greater importance to us both. We require somewhere new in London in which to reside with our governess Mistress Calthorpe. The King would no doubt be greatly indebted were your father to allow us to take up residence in Durham House, since by such means I would be able to maintain my visits to him.'

'It wants only the asking and it shall be done!' Guildford exclaimed, relieved that he would, by these simple means, achieve the double advantage of having Jane closer to him on a daily basis and being able to convey to his father something to the detriment of Thomas Seymour, against whom Sir John seemed recently to have taken a considerable dislike.

In the excited chatter that followed, it was agreed that the two young men would take their leave immediately and return with the family coach that would convey the two girls, their governess and all their baggage, the short distance to the Dudley family house in the The Strand that would become their new accommodation.

As they began to walk briskly back towards the house, Allan Bestwick hung back and Grace turned, then stopped and walked back towards him.

'Why are you delaying, Allan?' she asked as she looked more closely at the puzzled and yet somehow hopeful look on his face.

'I can readily understand,' he replied, 'why Lady Jane would be anxious to remain here in London, since by this means she may continue in her regular concourse with King Edward. But what reason might you have for wishing to remain?'

This stopped Grace in her tracks temporarily, since she had not stopped to analyse her motives. Anxious to prevent her face turning any pinker, she replied hastily, 'Jane is my friend — my only friend. Back in Leicestershire I would have no-one else to share my days with. Also, our governess is not as young as she once was and she would no doubt welcome my extra presence to preserve Jane's good name. Why, what other reason did you think there might be?'

'I thought perhaps...' Allan began hesitantly, then saw the encouraging grin on Grace's face. 'Perhaps — me?'

'Of course, you, Allan,' Grace said, as she looked behind her, then leaned forward and pecked his cheek.

XIII

The next few months passed blissfully, with both girls richly accommodated within the spacious confines of Durham House. Jane was increasingly in attendance on the young King Edward, while during her absence Grace was learning, from Allan, the finer points of horse maintenance and shoeing in the stables that adjoined the main building. He made no secret of the fact that once he became 'Sir' Allan Bestwick he intended either to return to his home village and assume the management of his father's farrier's business or start another one of his own in an adjoining village.

King Edward asked Jane, during one of their afternoon audiences, why she and Grace had left the Seymour house and when Jane proved evasive, Edward clapped his hands in frustration and glared at her. 'You do not lie to your King, Jane! Is it true that Thomas Seymour was playing unwanted court to my sister Elizabeth?'

'I can only tell you what I heard, Edward, since I saw nothing. And it may all be the work of evil tongues.'

'Somehow I doubt it,' Edward replied with a frown. 'He is said to have pursued her to the house in Cheshunt to which she fled to avoid his attentions. She is now further removed, to her house at Hatfield, which the Lady Mary has ordered to be securely guarded, with instructions that Sir Thomas is not to be allowed beyond the gate. Now, tell me what transpired in Chelsea.'

Jane recounted what little she had heard, omitting Grace's sighting of him in his nightshirt, being expelled from Elizabeth's chambers. She emphasised once again that it was only second-hand knowledge and might be the product of malicious tittle-tattle.

'But is it true that as a result of these goings-on, Lady Catherine has retreated to Sudeley Castle alone?'

'She is hardly alone, Edward, since she took most of her attendant ladies with her and hired a midwife to accompany her.'

'But she is apart from her husband Seymour?'

'So far as I am aware.'

Edward sat deep in thought for a moment, then looked up at Jane. 'I would deem it a great favour if you would join Lady Catherine in her final few weeks before giving birth. She did so much for me while married to my father and it grieves me to think of her as being alone at this time, while her so-called husband makes a fool of himself by playing unwanted court to my sister Elizabeth. Would you journey to Sudeley and take the Lady Catherine my best love and good wishes for a successful childbirth? It is her first and I hear tell that these things can be difficult, even for younger women.'

'I'd be more than happy to keep her company, Edward, but it would mean that you and I would not have the pleasure of our regular meetings. And what of my governess and my companion Grace?'

'You must of course take them with you. For myself, I will naturally miss our happy meetings, but it is a sign of the love and regard in which I hold the Lady Catherine, that I would part with your gracious presence in order that she should have the benefit of it.'

Late that afternoon Jane returned to Durham House with news of the King's wish that she and Grace join Catherine Seymour in her Gloucestershire retreat. Grace was not altogether happy to be leaving Allan behind in London, but kept her counsel and agreed that of course she'd be happy to accompany Jane, along with Mary Calthorpe. There was some initial concern that the journey might be too much for their aging governess, now well into her sixties, until Sir John Dudley gallantly offered his coach for the journey, along with an escort of his son Guildford, his squire Allan Bestwick, and three of his armed retinue.

This was sufficient to put the smile back on Grace's face and four days later their coach rumbled through the dusty late summer gateway to Sudeley Castle, where a warm welcome awaited them all.

Catherine Seymour was now less than a month from her lying in and was overcome with tears when she heard that the girls had arrived at the request of the King. During their brief stay at Chelsea Manor she had grown particularly close to Jane, and the presence of her governess, who had a lifetime's experience of child delivery behind her, was an additional benefit.

After two days it was time for their escort to depart back to London and Grace stood unhappily on the south terrace of the house, looking mournfully down at the coach that was being drawn up at the front entrance, with Guildford Dudley issuing instructions to the coachman. She was peering over the four foot high parapet in vain for a final sight of Allan when she heard a footfall behind her and turned to see him standing there, looking slightly uncomfortable. After a lengthy silence with their eyes locked on each other, it was Allan who spoke first.

'Forgive me, but I could not leave without saying farewell and they said that you had gone up onto the terrace to watch the departure. Guildford is down there with Jane and ... well...'

'Well what, Allan?' Grace teased him.

'Will you remember me fondly when I am gone?'

'Why would I not?'

'I know of no reason, but I ... I'll miss you, Grace,' he finally mumbled.

'And I will miss you also,' Grace said, before looking round carefully and adding, 'And since there seems to be no-one else to view our parting, why don't you kiss me and stop looking so awkward?'

Allan rushed over and folded her in his arms before planting a hot kiss on her lips. It was the first she had ever experienced from the lips of a young man and the world seemed suspended for a moment before she pushed him gently away with a smile.

'Enough to see you on your way, Master Bestwick. I will remember you fondly and do you perform the same service for me. No frolicking with the kitchen girls in the stables.'

'I leave that to the stable grooms,' Allan said, before executing a most gentlemanly bow and taking his leave.

Thomas Seymour was experiencing an altogether less pleasant exchange with his nephew Edward, who had commanded his presence for reasons that required no imagination on Thomas's part.

'It is ungallant, unseemly, immoral and an insult to my stepmother, Uncle. What has overtaken your wits?'

'Of what do you speak?' Thomas offered hopefully, then regretted it as Edward thumped the arm of his chair in a manner that reminded Thomas only too well of the petulant temper that the late King was wont to display.

'You know of what I speak!' Edward yelled. 'Not only was it the talk of London and the sole topic of whispers behind raised hands here at Court, but now I have a letter from my sister Mary, complaining of what she calls "the wanton and immoral behaviour of my sister Elizabeth with a married man whose wife is about to be delivered of a child." To whom do you imagine she is referring, Uncle? How many married men of your acquaintance, whose wife is about to give birth, do you know who recently had access to the Lady Elizabeth? And why has my stepmother taken herself from your company in order to give birth well out of your presence?'

'It was horse-play only,' Thomas muttered in self-defence.

'What was only horse-play?' Edward demanded.

Thomas chose his words carefully. 'Thanks to that gaoler of a governess, poor Elizabeth knew of no light-hearted diversion. So I took pity on the poor girl and would play games with her once she retired for the night.'

'"Games", Uncle?' Edward demanded, red in the face. 'Pray advise me what "games" a grown man plays, dressed only in his nightshirt, with a girl of fourteen?'

'I would tickle her feet and on one occasion I chased her round her chamber and smacked her bottom when I caught her.'

'And she was presumably clad in only her nightgown?'

'Naturally, since she had retired to her bed.'

'Presumably you were clad in more than your night attire when you visited her at Cheshunt?'

'Naturally. And during such visits, we merely walked in the garden.'

'Where you were seen with your arm around her waist and she resting her head on your shoulder. More than once, it seems. This was reported to the Lady Mary, who was so incensed at what she, in her pious virtue, regarded as little less than a seduction, that she ordered Elizabeth back to Hatfield and doubled the guard as a protection against your further approach to her sister.'

'With all due respect to the Lady Mary, Edward, she has the soul of a nun and the imagination of a playwright. Were you to ask the Lady Elizabeth herself, she would freely confirm that there was nought of lewdness about our behaviour.'

'Of course she would,' Edward pointed out, 'since she fears our sister's wrath. You are hereby ordered to have no further communings with the Lady Elizabeth. None whatsoever. Not even so much as a letter of enquiry regarding her health. Am I understood?'

'Certainly, Edward.'

'Certainly, *Your Majesty*,' Edward corrected him in a warning tone, and Thomas repeated the phrase with his head bowed.

'To further ensure your good behaviour in that regard,' Edward continued, 'you are commanded to journey down to Sudeley, in order to be by the Lady Catherine's side when she delivers your child. Lady Jane Grey is already down there, so she does not lack friendly company, thanks to my efforts. But it is your place to be there also, and while you are safely in Gloucestershire, certain persons in Hertfordshire will be free of your unwanted attentions. And your loyal response to that command is?'

'Yes, Your Majesty,' Thomas muttered before being dismissed from the presence, cursing quietly under his breath all the way down the corridor to the rear entrance to Hampton Court Palace. It was clear, in his mind, that Edward was being forced into a life that contained little light relief and no worthwhile contact whatsoever with those of the opposite sex. He was obviously apprehensive of incurring the ire of his older sister and no longer had the comforting presence of Lady Jane, with whom he was quite possibly in love without realising it.

Well he, Thomas, would take steps to remedy that oversight and when he could finally demonstrate to his naive and over-protected nephew that he was master of his own destiny and could, as King, live his life precisely as he chose, the fortunes of one of his uncles might well rise much higher than those of the other.

But first he had to travel to Sudeley and pretend that he cared.

The unheralded arrival of Thomas Seymour at Sudeley threw the household into a flutter. Catherine gave orders that Thomas was to be provided with his own suite of rooms, preferably far away from hers, and she took Mary Calthorpe quietly to one side and instructed her to be doubly mindful of her duties to guard the two girls in her care from even the suspicion of immoral behaviour. Jane spent almost every day in Catherine's company anyway, while Grace would take a horse from the stables and, with an armed escort drawn from the Seymour household, demonstrate her growing enthusiasm for exploring the surrounding countryside on horseback, wondering in her more withdrawn moments whether the rolling Cotswold Hills by which Sudeley was surrounded were anything like the river meadows of Attenborough that Allan had described to her.

At the very end of August, Catherine went into labour and after some initial difficulty that Mary Calthorpe put down to the fact that she was giving birth for the first time at the age of thirty-six, she was delivered of a girl they called Mary. Her husband Thomas seemed to take an interest in the infant and would regularly attend at Catherine's bedside to enquire as to her health. When she had been incapable of rising from her childbed for four days, a worried Mary Calthorpe told Thomas that she suspected childbed fever and banned him from further attendance at Catherine's bedside. The only regular visitor she was allowed was Jane, who looked on with a feeling of helpless horror as she witnessed the daily decline of the lady who had been so generous towards her.

On the fifth day, Catherine held out a weak hand and grasped Jane's. 'When I am gone, will you see to the mourning?'

'Of course,' Jane replied tearfully, 'but no more talk of your death, I beg you.'

'It is all that there is left to talk about,' Catherine replied with a weak smile, 'and I do not grieve my passing. And neither will that snake Seymour, who married me for who I am and what I owned, all of which will be his on my death, when he will look for a new bride who is much younger and who can offer him more than mere wealth. Beware of his charm, Jane, for you may be the one he sets his designs upon.'

'Me?' Jane asked in astonishment. 'Why me, pray?'

Catherine smiled knowingly. 'You are comely and you are young flesh, which Seymour prefers. But even more importantly, you are a royal princess, through your mother. Her mother was the Princess Mary Tudor, the aunt of our current King and it was well known in those days that Mary was King Henry's favoured sister. King Edward has ever shown you preference and — forgive me, but you must be advised — there are rumours that he sees you as a royal bride when he comes fully into his own. Seymour knows that and will no doubt seek your hand ahead of any such betrothal. Do not ever doubt your attraction as a bride and do not undersell yourself to seducers like Seymour.'

When Jane fell silent, Catherine felt compelled to confide further in her.

'You need not grieve for my passing, since I am glad to be taken out of this life. I had four husbands, one of them a king, and now I leave a daughter to follow behind me. As for the husband I also leave, I fear that he will show her no love, but will regard her solely for the match that can be made for her when she is of age. I have sent word to Catherine Suffolk, asking that of the love she bears me she take the child into her household, and I would ask that you ensure that this occurs. As for my so-called husband, have nothing to do with him, and for the sake of your reputations take yourself and your friend Grace back under Warwick's protection without delay.'

The following day, the light of life faded from Catherine's face and Jane sat sobbing quietly, holding her cooling hand, with Mary Calthorpe's hand resting on her shoulder in a gesture of comfort. Grace also consoled her and assisted in the preparations for the funeral, at which, at Seymour's request, Jane acted as chief mourner. During the mourning period, an urgent despatch was sent to London and the day after the funeral the Dudley coach swept up the driveway of Sudeley, with Guildford and Allan riding proudly behind it at the head of a small contingent of armed men.

As they turned from stabling their horses, they saw Grace standing quietly to one side of the stable entrance. Guildford made his excuses and walked away after his formal acknowledgment, and Allan and Grace stood facing each other. Allan grinned and jerked his head backwards to where the horses were being rubbed down.

'I trust that you did not frolic with the stable grooms in my absence?'

'I am no kitchen girl,' Grace replied. 'But welcome back, Allan Bestwick, and pray remind me of what I have been missing.'

As Guildford was bowing his respects to Jane at the front door to which she had come to welcome his return, he saw her eyes widening in shocked surprise as she looked over his shoulder. He turned and saw Grace and Allan in a tight embrace, followed by a lingering kiss.

'I believe that they get on quite well together,' Guildford observed laconically.

XIV

It was a clear, cold, moonlit January night, three months after Catherine Seymour's funeral, as Thomas Seymour alighted from the private wherry he had commissioned, with a whispered request for the wherryman to await his return. He worked his way through the ornamental privy garden that led from the Thames up the gentle slope towards the ground floor apartments of Hampton Court Palace that housed King Edward, scuttling between hedges and statues, flitting from shadow to shadow as he worked his way towards, and finally under, the walls.

There was a flower bed between him and the casement window that he knew could be forced with the metal bar that was tucked into the belt of his tunic, along with a pistol. As he stepped gingerly into the flower bed in his cautious approach to the window that, by his calculation, gave access to King Edward's bedchamber, there was a flurry of movement near his feet and a growl, followed by a sharp bark. His nerves screwed up to breaking point, Thomas drew his pistol and fired and with a pitiful whine the royal Spaniel puppy rolled onto its side and died.

Suddenly Thomas was surrounded on all sides by hulking shadows armed with halberds, swords and daggers, calling upon him to drop his weapon or else he would be run through a dozen times. As he stopped and raised his hands high in the air, throwing his pistol onto the path behind him, someone produced a lantern whose light temporarily blinded him, while a voice called out, 'That's him! That's Seymour! Hold the traitor!'

As they led him towards the south gate and the dungeon, he cursed his own incompetence. When news ran riot through the guardhouse, thence to the kitchens and from there to the bedchambers and audience rooms and out into the London streets, that Baron Seymour of Sudeley had been caught in the act of an attempt on the King's life, only John Dudley, Earl of Warwick, had to feign surprise.

Long before Edward Seymour arrived, the rest of the Council had agreed, with the King's enthusiastic consent, that the enquiry into Thomas Seymour's undoubted attempt on King Edward's life should be conducted by Thomas Wriothesley. For one thing, he was a trained and experienced lawyer, and for another he clearly had no love for the Seymours, one of whom had been instrumental is his dismissal as Lord Chancellor and the other of whom — the one under investigation and in peril of his life — had only ever treated him with contempt.

He was also known to be an unrepentant Catholic and therefore opposed to the Seymour faction who dominated the Council and the tutors responsible for the King's education. This made him trusted by the Lady Mary, who had penned one furious missive after another to London when she heard, third-hand, of what was widely believed to have been an attempt on Edward's life by an upstart philanderer who had made attempts on the virtue of her younger sister Elizabeth, no doubt as the result of all the lewd and licentious tendencies of the Protestant beliefs by which her childhood had been polluted. Mary was also demanding that the possible involvement of Elizabeth herself in the plot be investigated to its fullest and no-one but the pious and vinegar-faced

Wriothesley would be able to satisfy her that the task had been undertaken with sufficient thoroughness.

Edward Seymour was advised of the decision as soon as he arrived, late, at Council and he nodded without any attempt at argument. He had come to regard his brother Thomas as an embarrassment and a threat to his own continued dominance of affairs in Council, and his wife, for one, would rejoice when Thomas went to the scaffold, as he seemed destined to do. Being found at night with a loaded firearm, only feet from where the King was lying asleep, required a great deal of explaining away and so far there had been no such explanation.

The Council meeting resolved to attaint Thomas on multiple charges of treason that required no trial ahead of an execution that would follow as a matter of course. Edward Seymour listened solemnly to the King's litany of examples of Thomas's failure to obey his commands, his attempts to bribe Edward with money and gifts, his flirtations with Lady Elizabeth while his wife was burdened with pregnancy, and his open jealousy of the success of his older brother.

'The Earl of Southampton, my Lady.'

Princess Elizabeth rose from her needlepoint and indicated the chair next to hers, while calling for wine to be served.

'Sir Thomas,' she asked politely, 'to what do I owe this unexpected visit?'

Wriothesley was not one for the indirect approach, which perhaps accounted for his relative failure to acquire — or to retain for any length of time — high office in a Court that favoured forked tongues.

'You were presumably advised that Thomas Seymour was executed for treason?'

'Indeed, and my heart grieved to hear it,' Elizabeth replied innocently, unaware of the perilous ground she was treading.

'Did it indeed?' Wriothesley asked as his face set in displeasure. 'Could that be because of a certain affection that had arisen between the two of you?'

Suddenly Elizabeth became alert to the danger. 'Affection in what way, Sir Thomas? Certainly I was very much in his debt for the opportunity to reside in his house in Chelsea, where I could be closer to my dear friend the Queen Dowager and occasionally be granted audience with my dear brother.'

'And how was that debt repaid, madam?'

'I'm not sure that it ever was,' Elizabeth replied evasively, but Wriothesley was too much of a lawyer to allow her to wriggle that loosely.

'Not even by way of the natural affection of a young female to someone old enough to be her father?'

'To what do you allude, Master Wriothesley, because for the life of me I cannot fathom your meaning.'

'You kissed him?'

'On the cheek, occasionally, on the occasion of our arrivals and departures.'

'You allowed him to visit your bedchamber?'

'He was present on several occasions, certainly, as was my governess, who can give good account of what transpired.'

'Given that something "transpired", to employ your description, why should it be necessary for your governess to give "good account" of it — again your words?'

'Because,' Elizabeth replied haughtily after drawing a full breath for effect, 'it would seem from your questions that there might be some suggestion that it was other than seemly. It is well known that you are seeking evidence against Thomas Seymour to justify his execution, after the event it would seem, but I can save you further expenditure of breath by assuring you that you will hear nothing from me that will assist your mission.'

'My mission concerns more than the fate of Seymour,' Wriothesley replied ominously. 'It is believed that even he, foolhardy idiot that he always was, did not act of his own volition, since the crown was not his to gain. He was not of royal lineage and it is believed by some that his actions were intended to benefit someone who is — someone who had perhaps inflamed his passions with thoughts of lust beneath queenly sheets.'

Elizabeth almost laughed out loud, but instead opted for cool sarcasm. 'It is as well that the nation is not governed by those with such wild imaginations, Sir Thomas. Nor, with all the love that I bear my sister, could I contemplate for one moment that she could so inspire a man such as Thomas Seymour, who was probably sampling more carnal beauty long ere he attained manhood.'

'What put it into your mind that I might be referring to the Lady Mary?' was Wriothesley's next penetration question, to which Elizabeth shrugged.

'Who else could it have been? There is only myself of the royal line, apart from Mary and since it was not me, then could you perhaps be referring to the Lady Jane Grey, who is somewhere in the line behind me?'

'Do you deny that Thomas Seymour visited your bed chamber dressed only in his nightshirt?'

'Since his nightshirt was down below his knees,' Elizabeth replied flippantly, suppressing a giggle at the memory, 'then I cannot of course be sure that there was nought underneath.'

'And were you, at that time, dressed for bed?' Wriothesley persevered.

Elizabeth realised with some relish that she was beginning to shake his stern resolve. 'Since it was my bedchamber, I would hardly be dressed for the hunt,' she replied sarcastically.

'What transpired thereafter?' Wriothesley demanded.

'I went to sleep.'

'With Thomas Seymour?'

'Of course not. After he was chased from my bedchamber by my governess.'

'And what gave her cause to take such action?'

'That you must enquire of her, since I do not inhabit her mind.'

'This dissemblance does you no great honour, my Lady.'

'I do not dissemble. You are asking the questions and I am answering them as well as I am able. If the answers are not to your liking, that is hardly dissemblance. Rather, it smells of the truth, which I suspect is not what you came here in search of.'

'I shall speak with your governess.'

'And I shall see to it that you are accommodated in that desire. Are we finished?'

'For the time being only. And so I take my leave, my Lady.'

He bowed stiffly from the presence and once the chamber door was firmly shut behind him, Elizabeth allowed herself a long exhalation of breath to release the tension.

'He tickled her feet, then he slapped her backside,' the now-married Kat Ashley admitted to Thomas Wriothesley with a red face.

'Do you not agree that for a governess to allow that to happen to a girl of fourteen under her care was a gross dereliction of duty, compounded all the more because the girl in question is heir to the throne of England?'

'For all I know, it was merely in jest — a game,' Kat replied defensively. 'By all means take the same view that I have already heard third-hand from the Lady Mary, but I cannot say that there was aught in it that smacked of bawdy or licentiousness.'

'A girl of fourteen and a man of almost forty years?' Wriothesley asked cynically.

Kat sighed. 'I pity men of your age, Master Wriothesley, that they are capable of imagining themselves still attractive to young girls. As for my Lady Elizabeth, I have no doubt that she is capable of much greater discernment than to be attracted by wilting old flesh.'

'So you say that Thomas Seymour was not likely to have been performing his treasonous act at the urgings of the Lady Elizabeth?' Wriothesley asked.

'You did not ask me that question directly before, my Lord, but my answer would have been the same as that I give you now. Not only is my Lady Elizabeth not given to any carnal pursuits, not even minor ones, not only was she in no way sexually attracted to Sir Thomas, but in no way would she betray her natural love and regard for King Edward, her brother.'

'And so I take my leave, Mistress Ashley.'

'And not before time, Master Wriothesley.'

'She was in league with Seymour, of that I am convinced,' Lady Mary insisted as Thomas Wriothesley stood reverently before her in her Audience Chamber at Hunsdon House, not having yet been invited to take a seat.

'She denies that, as does her governess, my Lady,' Wriothesley told her softly, mentally bracing for the bad-tempered response.

'Of course they deny it, Wriothesley,' Mary replied in cold, clipped tones. 'Did you ever know a traitor admit guilt without torture, knowing the fate of traitors?'

'My Lady,' Wriothesley whispered, sick to the stomach, 'you cannot mean —'

'Do not presume to tell me what I can and cannot, mean, Wriothesley,' Mary barked commandingly. 'Just tell me what more you propose to do to explore the depths of this conspiracy against the true succession.'

'We cannot be sure that Seymour acted on anything other than his own urging, my Lady,' Wriothesley assured her, only to be wilted where he stood by a baleful glare.

'That idiot Seymour was fit only for managing a whorehouse. Can you seriously stand there and contend that he did not have the benefit of another's brain? His own did not rise above the cods, or so I am informed.'

'While you are undoubtedly correct in your assessment of the traitor Seymour, my Lady, that does not assist in identifying whose might have been the brain that he borrowed.'

'Obviously someone who sought to inherit the crown on Edward's death, you cretin! I thought I had instructed you to unearth that person.'

'In truth, my Lady, it was His Majesty who instructed me to enquire into the whole affair.'

'But it was I who alerted him to the distinct prospect that Seymour was urged on by others. And Kat Ashley has admitted that he was intimate with my sister Elizabeth, has she not?'

'I may have misunderstood what she said, my Lady. The word "intimate" was never employed by Mistress Ashley — she merely suggested that there may have been a little horseplay.'

'Have you ever known horses tickle each other's feet, Wriothesley? Or, for that matter, smack each other on their rear ends? Mistress Ashley is to be commended for her loyalty, but that hardly makes her testimony any more reliable. I do not suggest that you have her put to the question, but all the same she must be more severely questioned.'

Wriothesley's gut heaved at the prospect of the genteel Kat Ashley being tortured in order to wring from her what Mary clearly wished to hear, but was probably far from the truth and he sought to divert matters. 'The Lady Elizabeth was not, of course, the only female residing with the Seymours at around the time when any plot could have been hatched.'

'You are surely not suggesting the Lady Catherine herself?' Mary retorted contemptuously. 'Think, man! She had already been Queen, she was already wealthy beyond avarice and she was carrying a child!'

'I was referring to the Lady Jane, my Lady.'

Mary thought for a moment and her stern face set even more resolutely. 'You may be right, Wriothesley. She is of royal lineage, although well behind myself and the Lady Elizabeth, should Edward be no more. And given that she is only a few years younger than Elizabeth, she would, in the ordinary course of things, be an old woman ere the crown became hers, even assuming that neither I nor Elizabeth are blessed with offspring. Have you questioned her yet?'

'Not as such, no, my Lady, since she is reported to have been at Sudeley when the attempt on the King's life occurred.'

'That does not mean that she was not the one who urged Seymour to the deed when she was residing with him in London. The old goat was ever attracted to young flesh. And what better for her, than to be hidden away in the country and free from any suspicion of complicity in the deed itself?'

'You wish me to interrogate her, my Lady?'

'I wish you to unearth everyone involved in this dastardly plot — did I not make that clear from the outset?'

'If indeed it was a plot, my Lady.'

'Believe me, Wriothesley, it was a plot. Seymour would have been incapable of hatching anything so devious on his own. And when you have revealed who his conspirators were, they should all be put to the question. I shall be watching closely how you conduct this business, if I am not to conclude that you yourself were part of this treasonous attack on the line of succession. And since I am the next in line, I leave you to contemplate how seriously I regard this matter and how I will adjudge loyalty when the time comes to appoint my own senior advisers.'

The two girls looked apprehensively down through the lead mullioned window of the Great Hall on the first floor as a group of horsemen clattered in towards the stables of Durham House. The two girls had been anxiously waiting for news ever since Guildford and Allan had been sent to fight against a rebellion that had broken out against the King.

Jane let out a squeal of delight. 'They are led by Guildford!'

'I can't see Allan down there!' Grace wailed, then turned and ran down the staircase and into the stable yard in time to grab Guildford's tunic sleeve as he emerged from the stables. 'Is Allan with you?' she asked breathlessly, the tears starting in her eyes.

Guildford took both her hands in his and smiled. 'Have no fear, Mistress. He was alive when last I saw him and I would take a guess that he is less than half a day behind me. But I must return with my father and more soldiers, if we are to put down this rebellion.'

He had barely finished speaking when Grace was pushed roughly aside by Jane, who threw her arms around Guildford and hugged him tightly. 'Thank God!' she croaked though her tears, just as Sir John emerged from the house and walked swiftly across to Guildford.

'The time has come for me to save the day?' he asked of Guildford, who nodded.

'The royal army has fallen back on Cambridge and we need to regain Norwich.'

'We leave at daybreak tomorrow,' Sir John told him. 'But we go by way of Leicestershire.'

'You are taking us home?' Jane asked. 'Are we not safer here?'

'From armed rebellion, certainly,' Dudley replied, 'but not from smallpox. I have just returned from Council. There is another outbreak here in London and they say that King Edward has caught it this time and may not see the end of the week.'

XV

After two weeks back in Knighton with Mary Calthorpe, Grace was in two minds whether having a younger brother was a good thing or not. Thomas was now seven and very lively and inquisitive, which meant that in addition to her duties at Bradgate in respect of Jane, Catherine and Mary Grey, her Nanny had less time on her hands to supervise what Grace was up to as she roamed the modest estate and the countryside that surrounded it. That was obviously a benefit to Grace, but Thomas could also be very annoying and one of his great delights seemed to be tormenting his eleven-year-old sister. He had put more than one frog down the front of her bodice and was particularly accurate when it came to launching dried mud from some sort of home-made catapult.

He was also very keen on soliciting bribes, as Grace discovered on the very day of her return. They had spent three days on the road from London, bumping and swaying in the Dudley family coach along dry and dusty Midlands roads with a modest armed escort led by Sir John himself, with a saddle-weary Allan by his side, leaving Guildford to lead the main army back to Cambridge. They had stopped off first at Knighton, which lay to the south of Bradgate, and Grace and Jane had made their brief temporary farewells after Grace promised to coax her father into a visit within the week. Then the Dudley escort had headed north on the final delivery of Jane back to her parents, but not before a very mischievous Thomas had hidden behind the cattle barn on the Ashton estate while Grace bid a tearful farewell to Allan, who was again heading for the uncertainty of battle.

This farewell was intended to be a private one, out of full view of the manor house. Ordinarily the side of the cattle barn furthest away from the house could have been guaranteed to ensure them some privacy as they kissed and hugged each other with the growing passion to which each of them was rapidly succumbing, but they had failed to allow for the possibility that a mischievous seven-year-old had sneaked around the back.

Allan had not been gone more than an hour when Thomas gleefully informed Grace what he had witnessed and was even able to repeat a particularly embarrassing part of their conversation.

'I'll tell Mother and Father,' he threatened.

'And why should I care if you do tell them?' Grace demanded. 'Go ahead and see if it causes me any concern.'

Thomas slouched off and Grace dismissed his threat as a boyish prank until the following morning, when she was sitting watching the sheep being led back into the enclosure after they had been shorn. The bench in front of the manor house was meant to hold several people and her mother Kate sidled into the seat next to Grace and took her hand.

'Is it good to be home?' she asked.

Grace nodded without taking her eyes off the sheep. 'Yes, it is. It was busy enough in London for Jane, as usual, always going backwards and forwards to visit the King, but I had little enough to do unless the Lady Elizabeth was indoors and we could talk about her horses and things.'

'But you had a young man to occupy your interest, did you not?'

'Who might that be?' Grace asked in an attempted evasion, as her heart sank with the realisation that Thomas must have carried out his threat.

'Your brother tells me that there was a young soldier in the party that escorted you back here and that he saw you and he kissing just before he departed. Why would you not want us to know about this young man, Grace? Is there something about him that you wish to keep hidden from your parents? Let me guess, you imagine that we will object to your relationship because we believe him not to be good enough for you. Is that the reason for your reluctance to let us know of his place in your affections?'

'Yes,' Grace conceded.

Kate squeezed her hand. 'How will we ever know if he's good enough for you, if we know nothing about him?'

'Do you want to?'

'Of course, darling child, since he's obviously important to you.'

'His name's Allan Bestwick and he comes from a place called "Attenborough", which is only a day's ride north of here, on the banks of the River Trent. He comes from a large family and his father's a farrier, but he's a squire to Sir John Dudley and he hopes to be a knight one day, but of course there's always the risk that he'll be killed in battle. He's riding with Sir John to put down a rebellion in Norwich and I don't know if he'll ever come back alive and ... well and... Oh, he will come back safe, won't he?' Grace's voice cracked at this point and the tears began to collect behind her eyes as Kate put her arm round her and kissed her gently on the cheek.

'I think that you've convinced me that he's important to you, which is perhaps as well if you allow him to kiss you. But how does he feel about you?'

'I think that he may love me,' Grace replied.

'Well, if the two of you have genuine affection for each other, why should your father and I object?'

'Because,' Grace replied uncertainly, 'he's only a squire at present, with nothing to offer a wife.'

'Other than love and support, you mean?' Kate teased her. 'And why are you thinking in terms of marriage at only eleven years old?'

'Perhaps not marriage — not yet anyway,' Grace conceded. 'But even in years to come, what is he likely to have to offer the daughter of an estate?'

'And you think that your father and I would object, purely on that ground, if he's a good man and true and respects you and is faithful to you?'

'But I've seen life in London,' Grace argued, 'and Jane tells me all about the goings on at Court, where the conversation is all about wealth and estates and titles and suchlike.'

'I think you need to have a long conversation with your father,' Kate replied. 'Now come inside and eat some of the breakfast you left untouched.'

Two days later, Richard Ashton smiled at Grace across the breakfast table and asked, 'Do you think you could handle riding Patience for two hours or so today? One hour there and one hour back?'

Patience was a young filly born to one of the estate brood mares while Grace had been away. She'd been broken to human command and Grace had already happily walked her around the home paddock without mishap, so she nodded gleefully at the prospect of a longer ride on her back. 'Of course — where are we going?'

'To somewhere very important, in the ruins of Leicester Abbey.'

'The Cardinal's grave?' Thomas chipped in. 'That's boring!'

'Then you won't be disappointed when I tell you that you're not coming with us,' their father said. 'It's time that Grace learned how we come to be living here. Dress for a long ride, by your standards, Grace, and be prepared to do some rough gardening when we get there.'

Two hours later they stood on either side of a weed-strewn mound of earth, surrounded on all sides by the ruins of what had once been a large monastery, but had over the years been robbed of its finest stones following its closure along with most others of its type. At the head of the mound was a fine carved headstone and as Grace carefully fingered the moss in order to trace the inscription she looked across at her father.

'Why is the Cardinal's the only grave that's still properly tended?' she asked.

'It's been my life's work to maintain it in some semblance of decency. I've been coming here almost every week since before you were born, to keep down the weeds and it was in return for undertaking that service that I was granted our estate.'

'By the King?'

'No, the man in whose service I was at the time. You've heard of Thomas Cromwell?'

'I have,' Grace replied guardedly, 'but not always in a good way. Lady Mary says that he was a Godless heretic.'

'That's because he put an end to abbeys such as this one, which were an important part of the old religion that Lady Mary still espouses. But Cromwell was King Henry's Secretary and I was one of his clerks.'

'Only a clerk?' Grace asked with raised eyebrows. 'Then why did he give you this estate?'

'You need know nothing other than that I received it in return for tending this grave, which contains the body of Cardinal Thomas Wolsey, who rose from being the son of a butcher to become the most powerful man in England after the King. And he raised Thomas Cromwell to greatness — the son of a Putney blacksmith.'

'They both rose to high office, even though they were lowly born?' Grace queried.

Her father nodded. 'They were men of great ability and King Henry valued that. It made no difference to him that they did not come from a noble family, raised on a mighty estate.'

Grace looked thoughtfully across the mound at him. 'Did Mother tell you about Allan Bestwick?'

'She did indeed, and that's why I brought you here. Men of lowly birth can — and should — be judged by what they are and not where they come from. Now help me clear some of this marsh grass and let us respect the memory of a great man.'

As they rode back during the late afternoon, Grace had a few more questions. 'If men are to be judged by what they are, is it possible for the high born to be held down, despite their origins?'

'Indeed it is,' Richard said. 'I believe that the mighty Duke of Norfolk learned that hard lesson when he over-reached himself in the matter of his son's coat of arms. He was ever Cromwell's enemy — and therefore mine — but he's spent the past year or two as a prisoner in the Tower.'

'Why was he your enemy?'

'Because I worked for Cromwell, of course. And because I refused to lend my name to a rebellion he was planning against King Henry.'

'Your name must have been important to him. Were you once high-born, Father? I know nothing of your past.'

'It would be better if you didn't, but you may assume that my birth right was something of considerable significance to men like Norfolk. But I saw enough of the intrigues and back-stabbing at Court to want no more of it, which is why I settled for a humble estate as far from London as possible, where hopefully I may live out my days in peaceful obscurity. And I wish the same for you, unless the glamour of Court has already worked its fatal charm on you.'

'No, Father, I leave that sort of thing to Jane, who I must visit soon, in case she thinks I have forgotten her. But for me, perhaps a life married to a farrier on the banks of the Trent?'

'That remains to be seen,' Richard said. 'Remember that you are not yet even twelve.'

'How old was Mother when you first met her?'

'Enough questions. Concentrate on keeping your fine filly on the track ahead.'

XVI

'The Earl of Warwick, Your Majesty.'

John Dudley walked the short length to the raised throne, which looked ridiculously large with the diminutive figure almost lost inside it and made a sweeping bow.

'You have put down the rebellion?' Edward asked.

Dudley nodded. 'With considerable ease, Your Majesty, and over forty rebels are now hanging from Norwich's walls.'

'Well done, Warwick,' Edward replied, before giving way to a bout of coughing, then dabbing the phlegm from his chin.

'You are still unwell, Your Majesty?' Dudley asked solicitously.

Edward shook his head defiantly. 'It is merely a leftover from my recent malady. I was lucky to escape the worst of the smallpox that took so many in the city. The miasma here in Greenwich is not so perilous, it would seem. And I cannot afford to be ill, with so many rebellions around the nation.'

'Where do you wish me to take my men next, Your Majesty?'

'That would seem to be a waste of effort,' Edward replied. 'As fast as you cut down one clump of weeds, it seems that another springs up somewhere else in my realm. Traitors step in and whip the mob into a frenzy regarding small grievances, most of them religious. What we need are more sensible policies regarding the governance of the nation, not more bloodshed, which seems to breed only further resentment.'

'As a mere soldier, I can only offer armed suppression,' Dudley admitted.

'I think you are capable of more than that, my Lord Warwick, and I wish you to put down your sword and polish your diplomacy.'

'You wish me to travel to a foreign land, Your Majesty?'

'In one sense, yes,' Edward replied with a sour face, followed by further coughs and further wiping of the royal chin. 'I wish you to lend your wise voice to those in Council who oppose those policies that seemed destined to inspire rebellion.'

'But surely, Majesty, my Lord Somerset...?'

'My uncle brings me only policies that inflame the popular resentment, Warwick. And since he claims to act in my best interests, often not even consulting the rest of Council, I am not to know if I am being offered the wisest counsel.'

'Perhaps if you were to attend each Council meeting in person, Your Majesty?'

Edward gave an impatient wave of his hand and broke into more coughing. By the time that this latest attack had subsided, Dudley was already making mental plans.

'I do not attend many Council meetings, as you are well aware,' Edward reminded him. 'There are two reasons for that. One is that they bore me to distraction and the other is that I am not well placed to know which policy is the best and my uncle seems to carry the majority with him, principally because, as Lord Protector, he is able to overawe some and bribe others, to his point of view. Not always a wise point of view, as recent events have demonstrated.'

'So what do you desire of me?' Dudley asked, pretending a naivety that he had never possessed. 'Somerset is Lord Protector, with power to make policy without resort to Council.'

Edward smiled. 'He only acts without Council because I allow it. I intend to require him to put everything through

Council and then I wish you to lead the opposition to his proposals.'

'Even if they are wise?'

'We shall never know if they are wise unless they are fully debated, shall we? At present there are several members of Council who seek to counsel against certain proposals of my uncle's, but they are always in isolation and there is no-one with the courage to lead them and force the issue into wider debate. I wish you to be that person.'

'You wish me to lead opposition to every one of Somerset's proposed policies?'

'Precisely. There may be times when the majority are against you, but I suspect that once the more timid members of Council can see that you are their champion, they will take heart and push harder for full discussion, at the end of which every proposal of my uncle's will have been tested by strong argument and not simply agreed because he insists.'

'You ask a great deal of a mere soldier,' Dudley pointed out.

Edward nodded. 'But I do not ask it of you in your current rank, Sir John. For some time we have had no Earl of Northumberland worthy of the name. Given your recent military success, what could be more natural than for me to bestow that honour on you? Would you accept the title of Duke of Northumberland?'

'Gladly, Your Majesty,' Dudley said.

'This is all to the good, since it will give you added weight in Council, where I expect you to begin work without delay. Now leave me and be reunited with your family.'

By the end of that month, Edward Seymour could smell his own impending downfall. The boy King who had been content to accept whatever policy he brought to him was now insisting that he would not do so unless it was in writing and signed by every member of Council. Almost as a matter of course, Wriothesley, Earl of Southampton, Archbishop Cranmer and Fitzalan, Earl of Arundel, refused to add their names until there had been full debate, and the loudest voice against any policy that sought merely to appease rebels at the expense of the landed gentry and nobility came from the newly created Duke of Northumberland.

It came to a head three meetings later, when a stubborn minority in Council were refusing to put their names to a Bill that Edward Seymour had proposed. As tempers rose, Archbishop Cranmer suggested an adjournment to allow tempers to cool.

As the Council members left, Dudley smiled at Cranmer. 'My thanks, my Lord Archbishop. It would seem that my Lord of Somerset does not take well to organised opposition.'

'He is not used to it, that is why,' Cranmer said. 'But there is something related to the succession of which you should be aware, in case there be truth in the allegations regarding the Seymour ambition that led Thomas to the block while you were away in Norwich.'

Dudley sat down and motioned for Cranmer to take the seat next to his. 'Of what do you speak, your Grace?' he asked.

Cranmer's face became even more solemn. 'As you may not perhaps be aware, the King, in his youthful inexperience often relies on my advice during private audience. During his last illness he was convinced that he was dying and he dictated his dying wishes regarding the succession. If it be not amended before Edward dies — as die he must, of course, one day — then it has the potential to plunge the nation into civil war.'

'How?'

'In his own will, the late King Henry took the sensible course of devolving the crown first to Edward and his heirs, then to Mary and her heirs, then to Elizabeth and hers. He took no steps to legitimise their births and so they remain technically bastards. But out of an abundance of caution, he also added to the succession the descendants of his sister Mary, in order to prevent the crown going to any Scottish descendants of the other sister, Margaret. I believe he did so in a fit of pique because of the refusal of the Scots to betroth their own Queen Mary to Edward when he was still heir apparent.'

'And so?'

'This opened up the possible succession to the Grey family, but for some unaccountable reason Henry excluded his own niece Frances Grey and this left young Jane Grey in the line of succession.'

'So what has changed?'

Cranmer sighed. 'I tried to talk him out of it, but could only pursue my argument so far, since Edward's motives seem to have been religious in origin, and for that of course I must take much of the responsibility.'

'I would hazard a guess that he excluded the Lady Mary, who is still unrepentantly Catholic,' Dudley suggested.

Cranmer nodded. 'Indeed he did. But he also excluded Elizabeth, for the second reason he gave for excluding Mary, namely that they are both still adjudged bastards.'

'So if Edward were to die without heirs?'

'The crown goes to Jane Grey.'

Dudley was stunned by this revelation, but not enough to prevent his devious brain from considering the next steps he might take. 'Has the will been registered in any way?' he asked.

Cranmer shook his head. 'It is being copied to be issued as letters patent, which will require the consent of not only Council, but also the Parliament.'

'So at present it is known by the clerks of the Lord Chancellor's office, but no-one else?'

'Correct. And I believe that I can delay its publication while Edward lives. But of course, should Edward die heirless, it will come in due course before Council and I need hardly emphasise the uproar it will provoke among the remaining Catholics such as Wriothesley. Thank God that Norfolk is still in the Tower and likely to see out his days there. But what steps will you take to avert a constitutional crisis?'

Dudley smiled reassuringly. 'Since Edward is still alive, we have time. Time which I can use to my advantage.'

XVII

Edward Seymour, Duke of Somerset, sat staring distractedly into the fire in the apartments he shared with his wife Anne at Greenwich Palace. Anne couldn't quite believe the change in his normally confident manner and put her needlepoint down on the table beside her chair opposite his by the fire and stared into his blank face. It was late January 1550 and she was glad of the warmth from the blazing logs, but the desolated look on Edward's countenance sent a chill right through her.

'What ails you?' she asked tentatively, not confident of any meaningful response.

'Nought ails me — yet,' Edward muttered, 'but as for what is to come, who knows?'

'Your meaning?'

'I fear a plot.'

'Against you, or King Edward?'

'Is that not the same thing?' Edward replied testily. 'There is a mood abroad in Council that would seem to be aimed at undermining anything I suggest for the benefit of the realm and therefore its King. King Edward gives the appearance of going along with it, but I cannot be sure that he is not the dupe of others, most notably Dudley, who has now been elevated to the Dukedom of Northumberland.'

'What makes you suspect Dudley?'

'He was close with my brother shortly before his attempt on the King's life. Thomas may have gone to his death, but you know as well as I that the man was a mindless peacock. As for who was really behind the plot we can only conjecture, but it led almost immediately to Dudley's rise in the King's estimation.'

'Isn't Wriothesley charged with the duty of smoking out those who were behind the plot?' Anne asked. 'That being the case, why do you trouble your mind with it?'

Edward shot her an exasperated glare. 'Did I not just say that since the failure of the plot, Dudley has risen to favour in Edward's eyes, whereas I have fallen? I fear that my nephew has received secret but false counsel that I was somehow involved in Thomas's lunatic scheme.'

'From Dudley?'

'Who else? At the same time that Dudley's fortunes have risen, mine are being held down with King Edward's approval, if not his actual instruction. It is as if I am suspected of complicity in what Thomas did and I fear that Wriothesley has been quietly instructed to look no further than me for an explanation of how someone as famously brainless as Thomas could have contrived a bid for the crown. A crown, what is more, that could never have been his in the ordinary course of things.'

'But if it could never have become his, how can anyone argue that it could ever have become yours?' Anne replied. 'And if not, then what could you possibly have stood to gain by Edward's death?'

'If you were listening correctly, mind that I said "in the ordinary course of things"?'

'So?'

'So who was it who made such great effort to have the Lady Jane Grey residing in his house? And for what purpose, think you?'

'Knowing your brother Thomas and his taste for young girls, I dread to think,' Anne grimaced. 'His attachment to that fading baggage Catherine Parr was a surprise to anyone who knew him even vaguely — she was at least twenty years older than the age he preferred them.'

Edward sighed. 'Think, woman — and think beyond the obvious! Jane Grey has no beauty above average and Thomas had a ready supply of innocent young girls through his sickening patronage of several city orphanages. If not, then, her beauty, why did he go to the trouble of having her brought down from her father's estate three days' ride to the north?'

'It was to please King Edward, was it not?'

'That was the reason at first, yes. But then it became known — to members of the Council anyway — that Jane had been mentioned in Henry's succession. Given certain future events in her favour, she might one day aspire to be Queen.'

'So it is your belief that Thomas befriended Jane Grey in order, first to get closer to King Edward, and then stab him in the back and assist Jane to the throne? And for what reward? Her hand in marriage? Surely, not even a simple girl from the country would be so desperate?'

'She is far from simple, believe me,' Edward insisted, 'and Henry Grey's wife is ambitious for their daughter.'

'But now that Thomas is dead, surely any hope she might have had of stepping onto the throne is no better than it ever was? You forget the royal princesses Mary and Elizabeth, surely?'

'Were Edward to die before reaching maturity, the future of the realm would lie in the hands of Council,' Edward reminded her. 'The majority of them would be against Mary, because she would return us to Rome in her very first act as Queen. As for Elizabeth, she is barely fifteen and given to being frivolous and empty-headed, insofar as it is possible to read her. Compared with those two, even the thirteen-year-old Jane might be acceptable to a Council dominated by Dudley.'

'So why does King Edward give preference to Dudley, thereby promoting Jane's bid for an early crown, if you be correct?'

'Because he knows no better!' Edward shouted in frustration. 'All accounts are that Edward dotes on Jane, to the extent that it is rumoured that he sees her as his future bride when he comes into his own. She has played the long hand well and it wants only a few more years before she can probably seduce her way into Edward's bed anyway.'

'So she has no need to plot with Dudley?' Anne reasoned.

Edward frowned. 'We cannot be sure that she even plotted with Thomas, at least not directly,' he replied. 'I believe that it was Thomas's plan to offer her the crown once Edward was dead, using Dudley as his armed support. Now, with Thomas gone, Dudley has stepped to the forefront of the plot.'

'So does Dudley plot against Edward's life, or does he simply seek to continue to push Edward and Jane together and let love take its course?'

'That I do not know,' Edward admitted, 'which is why I gaze into the fire for answers. But either way, two things remain clear. One is that Dudley has gained supremacy in Council, with Edward's blessing, and the other is that Jane Grey is his master chess piece.'

'So what do you plan to do?'

Edward grimaced, then spat into the fire. 'Much though it irks me, I must ally myself with Wriothesley while he conducts his enquiries. He has no love for me, obviously, but the King has given him the task of unearthing those who were behind Thomas, while the Lady Mary is insisting that he point the finger of accusation at Lady Elizabeth. I must somehow divert Wriothesley's attentions towards the Grey girl.'

'And how will you do that?'

'First we must get her back to London, where she will be more available for questioning by Wriothesley. So I think that you and I must pay another visit to Bradgate.'

'This is intolerable!' Elizabeth protested as Wriothesley's entrance was announced. She was standing with her back to the roaring fire, hands on hips and her mouth set in an expression of displeasure.

'How so, madam?' Wriothesley enquired with his usual air of cool indifference.

'You have made a virtual prisoner of Mistress Ashley and you have confined several of my household to their rooms here at Hatfield. Several of them were not even in London with me, so how could they possibly know anything of my actions while in Baron Seymour's house?'

'Some of them, however, were with you during your stay with Sir Anthony Denny,' Wriothesley replied without seemingly moving a single face muscle. 'Mistress Parry, for example, who tells a pretty tale of your walks in the garden in Cheshunt on the arm of Thomas Seymour.'

'Walks, Wriothesley,' Elizabeth snarled. 'Walks only.'

'With his arm around your waist and your head on his shoulder?'

'If Blanche Parry was close enough behind us to hear aught of our conversations, then she no doubt advised you that we spoke largely of the health of my very good friend Catherine Parr — the former Queen, let me remind you — and her impending childbirth. Perhaps Blanche did not hear such trivial exchanges, or you were not able to terrify her into falsely revealing worse, but you cannot seriously suggest that I would be involved in some intrigue of the flesh with the husband of a very good friend who was carrying his child?'

'You stood to benefit from the death of King Edward, did you not?'

'He is not dead.'

'I speak hypothetically, madam. Were ought to befall King Edward, you would move closer to the throne of England, would you not?'

'Behind my sister Mary,' Elizabeth reminded him, at which he smiled.

'Even assuming that nothing untoward happened to the Lady Mary, she is still senior to you by some seventeen years and could be expected to die naturally while you were still in your prime. Edward, on the other hand, could well outlive you both.'

'Your meaning?'

'It suited you to have him out of the way.'

'As it also suited Mary — have you subjected her to the same indignities that you inflict upon me and my household? And when do you intend to desist?'

'When I have the truth, madam.'

'The actual truth, which I have already disclosed to you, or the version of the truth that is desired by yourself and my sister? Do you fondly imagine that I do not know who really saddles your horse, Master Wriothesley? Dear Edward would never give authority for me to be hounded in this way, whereas for Mary it would be merely consistent with the manner in which she has treated me since my birth. Return to Hunsdon, my Lord, and advise my loving sister that any "understanding" I might have had with Thomas Seymour existed only in her fevered imagination.'

'I shall of course be reporting all this,' Wriothesley sneered, 'including your seeming lack of enthusiasm for the revelation of all those behind the threat to the King's life. But first I must return to London and report all that I have learned so far.'

'Do not let me be the cause of your delay, Master Wriothesley,' Elizabeth said sarcastically, 'since presumably my household staff will now be free to discharge their normal duties. When you call in at Hundson on your return to London, be sure and give my sister my kind regards and assure her that my conscience is in no way afflicted.'

XVIII

'To what do I owe the honour, Uncle?' King Edward asked with a sneer as Edward Seymour bowed into his presense.

'Various reasons, Your Majesty. First, to enquire as to your health. Secondly, for news of any further progress by Master Wriothesley in his enquiries. And finally — and perhaps more welcome to your ears — to suggest that the Lady Jane Grey be invited back to Court, now that you appear to be returning to full health.'

'As for my health,' the King frowned, 'the agues have not completely left me and my physicians advise that these are the lingering legacies of the smallpox that recently beset our city. They advise more purgings and perhaps some country air.'

'Windsor?' Edward Seymour asked.

'Can it be made ready within the week? I own that life here at Greenwich has become even more tedious, now that fussing physicians have been added to my daily burden of tutors. I wonder that this was once regarded as a place of pleasure.'

'You are correct in your assertion that it is too close to the city, if you are to avoid the risk of common diseases that waft across on the river breezes.'

'You made mention of Lady Jane. Does she remain on her estate?'

'Indeed she does, Your Majesty, for fear of the recent contagions. But were you to transfer to Windsor, I would undertake to have her brought to you there, in order that you might renew your happy acquaintance.'

'Do it, Uncle, and earn my thanks.'

'May I enquire as to how Wriothesley's commission is faring? Council has been awaiting his first report for several months now and we are all naturally anxious that should there be any left in the plot against your life...'

'Yes, quite,' Edward interrupted him. 'Well, as you can see, I am still in this world and far from convinced that anyone other than a lunatic like your brother could possibly have had designs on my death. In fact, there are days when I doubt that even he meant to kill me.'

'And Wriothesley?'

'I expect him back daily, and please assure my Council that he will lose no time in making his report. Now, if there is nothing else, perhaps you would care to take yourself off to Leicestershire without delay?'

Five days later, at a Council meeting summoned to meet at Greenwich for the greater convenience of King Edward, Wriothesley presented his inconclusive report, to considerable dissatisfaction all round.

'In short, you are no nearer to revealing who else was involved?' Dudley demanded.

Wriothesley inclined his head in a respectful gesture as he replied, 'With the greatest respect to my Lord of Northumberland, it has only ever been *assumed* that there were others involved in the matter.'

'Wriothesley,' Edward Seymour responded with a sour face, 'even I, as the idiot's brother, have to concede that he would not have taken a single step on a course of action that a ten-year-old could have assured him was doomed to failure, unless he was persuaded to it by someone else.'

'Perhaps,' Archbishop Cranmer observed out loud, 'the object was not the death of the King, but the downfall of Thomas Seymour himself.'

'What evidence did you unearth that this might have been the case?' Dudley asked nervously of Wriothesley, who shrugged his shoulders.

'His Grace may be correct, in that I have so far interrogated everyone who might have been behind a plot against His Majesty, without detecting any suggestion of guilty conscience.'

'How about my sister Mary?' the King demanded. 'Surely, as the next in line under my father's will, she had the most to gain?'

'You would accuse your own sister, Your Majesty?'

'Why not, since according to letters of complaint that I receive almost daily from our other sister Elizabeth, you persecuted her and every member of her household, every day for a month?'

It fell silent, until Edward Seymour saw his opportunity. 'Perhaps the guilt lies elsewhere in the succession, Your Majesty?'

King Edward's face set in an angry scowl. 'You mean who, precisely?'

'Did not your father's dying succession wishes include the Lady Jane Grey?'

'Enough!' the King shouted, as his fist came down hard on the table. 'This search for those to blame for Seymour's seeming loss of wits has gone far enough! Wriothesley, see that the Clerk to Council has the final draft of your report and then discontinue your enquiries.'

'But, Your Majesty —' Wriothesley began to argue, before the royal fist again hit the table.

'You have your orders! You have failed in your mission, for reasons that may not lie entirely at your door, but that mission is now at an end. Am I understood?'

'Absolutely, Your Majesty.'

'Good. Now, what other items of business have we?'

Two hours later, as the Council dispersed, Edward Seymour sidled up to Thomas Wriothesley.

'I know that we have never been the closest of friends, Thomas,' Edward mumbled, 'but I am concerned that your mission has been terminated in this fashion. As Thomas's brother, I clearly feel a deep sense of family shame and would dearly love to learn who was behind his downfall.'

Wriothesley turned his head to regard Edward with a look of mingled suspicion and resentment. 'You robbed me of my Chancellorship. Why should I now assist you?'

'For my part, to in some way retrieve my family's good name. But for you, the opportunity to demonstrate to the King that you are capable of penetrating the most carefully woven web of treason.'

'You heard what I had to report to Council, Somerset. I have so far discovered no evidence of complicity on the part of anyone else.'

'Perhaps you have not been asking the right people.'

'Meaning?'

'Cranmer may have been correct that the entire object of the madcap scheme was to ensure the downfall of my brother Thomas. We must then ask who stood to gain by that downfall.'

'And your answer to your own question?'

'It is well known that at the time when Thomas was caught with a loaded weapon in the Hampton garden, his wife had transferred herself to Sudeley for her lying in.'

'Because she was disgusted by his behaviour with the Lady Elizabeth, or so I was informed.'

'And that information was correct, insofar as it went,' Edward reassured him. 'You have been assuming all along, have you not, that it was Elizabeth's desire for the crown that led her to seduce Thomas into his rash enterprise?'

'Indeed.'

'Well, Elizabeth was not the only young lady resident at Chelsea Manor at that time who had a claim on the throne should aught befall King Edward.'

'You mean the Lady Jane?' Wriothesley asked, horror-stricken.

'And why not?' Seymour persisted. 'She was resident there, she is just at that age when young girls have no control over their bodily urges or their fascination with older men, and my brother had a vile reputation with young girls. It may not have been Elizabeth with whom he hatched the plan, but the young girl Jane.'

'But you heard His Majesty's reaction when her name was merely mentioned in his presence as a possible conspirator with your brother.'

'Because young Edward is smitten with her. She would be the last person he would accept as having been behind a threat to his life, which makes her all the more dangerous should she attempt to dupe someone else into doing the deed. Someone more capable than my useless brother.'

'Who, for example?' Wriothesley asked, somewhat out of his depth when it came to conjecture rather than blunt accusation.

'When Catherine Seymour retired down to Sudeley, where did Lady Jane find alternative accommodation?'

'I have no idea, my Lord.'

'In Durham House, along with Dudley and his family.'

'You suspect Dudley's hand in all this?'

'That is for you to determine, Thomas. I merely offer it to you as a suggestion.'

'You seem to be ahead of me, Somerset. Explain carefully to me how you perceive matters to have lain.'

'I can only offer conjecture based upon the known facts. The first of those facts is that Lady Jane was resident in my brother's house in Chelsea, where either he seduced her, or she tempted him, on the urging of Dudley, into a foolhardy act that could only result in his downfall. This may either have been because Dudley wished to see the Seymours disgraced, in order to enjoy the dominance over Council that he now enjoys, or because Lady Jane was persuaded, in her country naivety, that she could become Queen of England. She then transferred to Dudley's house for safety, once your enquiry was commenced and then was able to use the convenient excuse of the outbreak of smallpox in order to retreat to her Leicestershire estate until the scandal subsided and Elizabeth became the convenient victim of Lady Mary's venom.'

'Think you that Jane has an unchaste passion for Dudley?'

'I do not care one way or the other, Thomas. I simply suggest that the names of Grey and Dudley may be linked to a plot against the throne and that you would be performing a great service to the nation — and of course the King himself — by revealing it.'

'And where, pray, would you recommend that I begin?'

'I have been able to take that first step for you, my friend in need. I have secured the King's consent to Lady Jane being brought back to Court, but at Windsor rather than here, too close to the miasmas that waft off the river. Once I have her down here, you may begin to subtly question her.'

'If she complains to King Edward, he will have my head!' Wriothesley protested.

'Not if you act from the pure motivation that has driven you thus far, Thomas. Or do you wish this matter to end with the conclusion that Master Wriothesley failed in a commission direct from the Crown?'

'Let me know once Lady Jane is accommodated at Windsor and I'll give the matter further thought,' Wriothesley promised, and departed with a furrowed brow, leaving Edward Seymour with a feeling of elation.

'Must I go without Grace?' Jane complained as they sat at supper, her lower lip quivering in a mixture of nervous defiance and impending tears. Her mother placed a reassuring hand on her shoulder.

'King Edward has been in poor health of late and it seems that you are one of the means by which he may be offered the prospect of recovery,' Lady Frances reminded her. 'At least, that's what the Duke of Somerset assures us and he has journeyed here specially to take you back with him at the King's request. How would it be regarded were you to refuse to travel to the side of your King in order to assist him back to full health?'

'But why can Grace not come with me?'

'Because,' her father told her, 'at thirteen years of age, it's time you faced life without the friend who was perhaps appropriate when you would climb trees and wade in the fish pond, but must now be put aside as you prepare to take your place at Court.'

'Even if I don't want to?' Jane pouted.

'Particularly if you don't want to,' Henry Grey insisted. 'To my mind, you've been indulged a little too much in the matter of childish pranks with our neighbours' daughter, but now you have to face up to the future that lies ahead of you, just as we all had to do in our time.'

'It was easy for you,' Jane complained, 'since Mother was the King's niece and her parents were at Court all the time, so she learned how to behave at her mother's knee. And up to now all I've done is sit and talk with King Edward, share his games, talk about his lessons and so on. Why does he want me to parade myself in the full Court, like some prize heifer at Leicester Market?'

'We can only pass on what the Duke of Somerset tells us,' her father replied. 'He'll be joining us for supper, of course, once he returns from his business in Knighton, and he can tell you all about what King Edward has in mind for you.'

'Why is he riding to Knighton?' Jane asked suspiciously. 'Will he be telling Grace that her friend's deserting her for a rich life at Court? She'll be heartbroken if she thinks I'm rejecting her in that way.'

'You'll obviously have ample time to explain matters to her in time to come,' her mother coaxed her, but Jane shook her striking red locks defiantly.

'How can I possibly explain it to her if I don't even understand it myself?' she complained. 'And what about Nanny Calthorpe?'

'Young ladies at Court don't require nannies,' Frances observed.

'This one will,' Jane insisted as the tears began to flow freely and her parents looked apprehensively at each other over her bowed head.

XIX

'Where are my normal guards and who are these people?' King Edward demanded sharply as Edward Seymour bowed into the presence.

Seymour smiled reassuringly. 'Given the recent threat to your life, I thought it better to install my own men, Your Majesty.'

'And what was wrong with the usual guard?' his nephew demanded testily. 'Did they not manage to apprehend my other uncle — the mad one — before he had got beyond the privy garden?'

'Only because they were alerted in advance, Your Majesty.'

'By whom?'

'I have no idea. I was given that information by the Captain of the Guard, but only after I questioned him most rigorously,' Seymour lied. 'I was not satisfied that I was getting the entire truth and would be much happier if my own men were responsible for your personal safety.'

'And where is the Lady Jane?'

'Outside, Majesty.'

'You left her waiting in the corridor?' King Edward bellowed in angry disbelief. 'Bring her in — now!'

A somewhat apprehensive Jane was called into the presence and Seymour slid back out through the double doors into the hallway.

King Edward noted Jane's dejected look immediately. 'My dear Jane,' he said consolingly, 'you look sad. Why is this, when we are reunited after so many months?'

'In truth, Edward,' she replied as she allowed the King to take her hand and led her to the chair next to his, 'I am fearful

135

that when I am formally presented at Court I will shame myself by being a country bumpkin with poor manners and ungracious actions. I will need time to prepare for my first appearance.'

Edward looked puzzled. 'Who told you that you were to be formally presented at Court?'

'The Duke of Somerset. At least, that's what he told my parents, seemingly.'

'He had no business saying that,' Edward assured her. 'There will of course come a time when you will be presented at Court, but not before you are ready. In truth, you are here solely in order to raise my spirits, which my physicians assure me will in due course improve my health. But enough of that — tell me how you have been these past few months, and how is Leicestershire?'

'Middling well, thank you, Edward, but I miss my lifelong friend, who was with me during my previous times in London, but has now been left behind, on the insistence of my parents.'

'Is she regarded by them as not suitable as a companion for you?'

'Only because they thought I was being presented at Court. If I am not, then perhaps I could send word for her to travel down here in order to be with me?'

'Of course you may, and without delay. What is her name?'

'You may remember her. Grace Ashton. She is the daughter of Sir Richard Ashton, who has a neighbouring estate to ours at Knighton. Grace and I grew up together and she is my dearest friend.'

'Then we should lose no time in having her brought down here to Windsor. The park here has excellent distractions and the surrounding countryside is most pleasing for brief excursions on horseback. Do you both ride?'

'After a fashion.'

'Then we should spend a few days ahead of her arrival reacquainting you with the delights of being on horseback. I'll give instructions for a quiet horse to be allocated to you from the stables here and we shall go riding tomorrow, after my lessons.'

The following morning, when Edward announced his desire to go riding along the distant Thames riverbank in the company of Jane, he was politely advised that Seymour had left word that, for his own safety, the King was not to proceed beyond the outer gate of Windsor Castle. Edward angrily summoned his uncle into his presence and demanded an explanation.

'It is for your own safety, Your Majesty, given the recent attack on your own life.'

'*Alleged* attack, Uncle. And is this *alleged* attack to be used as a justification for keeping me within the Castle walls like some captured foreign prince?'

'I am the Lord Protector as well as your uncle, Edward, and my first duty is to protect you and, by the same process, the line of succession.'

'And how will I attend Council? Or do you propose to bring the Council here, whenever we have need to convene it?'

'That is obviously one possible course of action, Your Majesty. The alternative would be for me to convey your wishes to Council in person and ensure that they are fulfilled.'

'And has Council yet agreed to either course?'

'Clearly not, since I have not yet put those options to them. Perhaps now might be the opportune moment for you to choose.'

'I choose to return to Greenwich, Uncle.'

'Given the ongoing risk to your person, I cannot allow that, Edward.'

'*Your Majesty*,' Edward insisted. 'And who are you, to decide what to allow me and what to keep me from?'

'I am the Lord Protector, Your Majesty, and even though you are my nephew and my King, my first duty is to the nation.'

'And should I choose to appoint another Lord Protector?'

'I was appointed by Council, it will be recalled.'

'A Council that you bribed!'

'Nevertheless, it would require the approval of Council to replace me.'

'Then summon Council here to Windsor and let us do precisely that.'

'As you wish, Your Majesty,' Seymour bowed with a sustained smirk. 'Once the weather is more favourable.'

'Now!' Edward bellowed, as he waved his uncle out of his presence and called for Jane, who entered, looking distressed.

'What ails you, Jane?' Edward asked.

She lowered her eyes as she slid into her usual chair and whispered, 'Why have you sent that awful man Wriothesley to ask me impertinent questions? Do you believe that I was involved in some way in the attack on your life, even though I was at that time attending the Lady Catherine at Sudeley?'

'I gave no such order, to Wriothesley or to anyone else. Say you that he accuses you of being in league with Thomas Seymour in his foolishness?'

'More or less. He asked about my "doings" with Seymour while we were all living under the same roof in Chelsea. He also wished to know what I saw of Seymour's "doings" with the Lady Elizabeth, and I was obliged to tell him. Have you brought me down here to be interrogated?'

'Of course not, dear Jane. I had no idea that Wriothesley was even here at Windsor, and I shall lose no time in having him sent back downriver. His commission was cancelled some time ago.'

'What commission?'

'You need not concern yourself with that. But since the alleged attack on my life, there have been many enquiries as to who might have been behind it, other than Thomas Seymour, that is. The older brother, who insists that he is the Lord Protector, and must therefore keep me confined here for the good of the nation, as if I were a prisoner, has clearly countermanded my order that Wriothesley pursue his enquiries no further. I seem no longer to be in command of the nation of which I am King.'

'Can you not simply command to be taken back to Greenwich, or perhaps Hampton?' Jane asked fearfully.

Edward shook his head and waved a hand in the general direction of the double doors to his audience chamber. 'The guards outside are all Seymour's men and they tell me — with excessive politeness — what I may and may not, do, beyond the walls of the Palace here.'

'So we are both prisoners?'

Edward nodded, then looked at her with widening eyes. 'But there is yet hope to get word to Council, which has not met recently, for various reasons that Somerset offers as lame excuses. Either it is the inclement weather, or the illness of Council members, or some such poor justification.'

'How do you propose to get word to them? Are your despatches read by Seymour or one of his bullies?'

'I know not. But it is unlikely that yours will be.'

'I know of no-one to whom I may write, I'm afraid,' Jane conceded.

Edward still had a gleam in his eye. 'Your friend in Leicestershire — the one you wished to have brought down here?'

'Grace Ashton?'

'Could you not write to her — perhaps in some sort of code known only to each of you — seemingly inviting her down here, but in truth asking that she gather an armed force to release us?'

Jane laughed, then corrected herself. 'Forgive me, Edward, but the only army that Grace Ashton would be likely to be able to raise would consist of sheep, goats and water fowl from her estate.'

'She has no friends in London in positions of armed power?'

'Only Sir John Dudley.'

'The Duke of Northumberland?' Edward asked. 'Do you tell me that Grace is friendly with Northumberland?'

'In truth, it is I who can better claim that,' Jane replied, 'since we both resided in his house at his invitation when Baron Seymour went to Sudeley. But my friend Grace is very friendly with Sir John's squire, and if I write to her, disguising my true message in some way, I'm sure she can alert Sir John and thereby arrange for his men to come and release us.'

Just over a week later, a puzzled Grace Ashton was reading and re-reading a portion of Jane's letter to her, inviting her down to Windsor Palace. Knowing Jane as well as she did, she felt certain that there was some hidden message in there and she had never before known Jane to write to her — in truth, it was one of the rare occasions when she had even seen Jane's very accomplished handwriting.

Eventually she opted for the opinion of someone whose superior intelligence and experience of life was readily available. She found her father in the stables, rubbing down his horse after his weekly pilgrimage to the Cardinal's grave, and she put her hand into his and smiled her winning smile. 'Father, I have this letter from Jane, as you know, but there is something in it that puzzles me. What would you make of this passage?'

She looked down at the vellum, now badly creased and repeated what Jane had written. 'I really miss you now that the games here at Windsor have grown more serious and the other Seymour insists that Edward and I play that game that you and I used to play in the milking parlour. Perhaps you should bring Guildford and his father to break up the game.'

'To what game is she referring?' Richard asked, at a loss to understand the oblique allusion.

'When the milking parlour was empty, we'd creep into one of the stalls and pile hay bales in front of it, so that it resembled a prison cell. Then we'd take it in turn to play "prisoner and gaoler". But why would she and King Edward be playing that game, and why should Guildford and his father be invited to end it?'

Richard looked into her eyes with a stern expression. 'This is not some childish game between you, designed to make me look foolish?'

'Of course not, Father — but what can it mean?'

'I think it means that you are required back in London as a matter of urgency. As I read this, Edward Seymour has Jane and the King imprisoned in Windsor Palace. Go and alert Maryy Calthorpe that we shall be leaving at first light tomorrow. We go first to Bradgate for some of Grey's retinue to accompany us, then we go to rescue our King. And, of course, your very clever friend.'

141

XX

'We must be very guarded in how we approach this,' John Dudley told the Ashtons as they sat around the supper table. Wine and wafers had appeared as if by magic and supper had been ordered an hour early when Richard Ashton revealed why they were there unannounced with an escort of men in the Grey livery.

'You share my unease regarding Jane's hidden message?' Richard asked.

Dudley shook his head. 'Not really, since the Lady Jane has always seemed to me to be a most intelligent girl for her age. Also, the nature of her message — and the careful way in which it was ciphered — further underlines her devotion to the truth. My concern is that we do not overreact.'

'But surely, if the King be imprisoned...' Richard began, then fell silent as Dudley raised his hand.

'There can be no doubt of that, in a general sense. He is being confined inside Windsor, certainly, but were I to challenge Somerset's actions, he would claim merely that Edward is being isolated from further contagion. That is the reason he has given these past few weeks for not summoning Council.'

'But that cannot, in the normal course of things, be allowed to continue, surely?' Guilford chimed in, despite his father's annoyed frown at his presumption. 'What I mean is that the Council is required to meet regularly for the governance of the nation.'

Dudley shook his head with a look of resignation. 'Somerset is "Lord Protector" and for some years has been authorised to make decisions without the consent — or even the knowledge — of Council. While he has King Edward contained, he can conduct the affairs of State as if he were King.'

'All the more reason why we should at least attempt to rescue Edward from his clutches,' Richard argued.

Dudley nodded. 'This must, of course, be our ultimate objective, but first we must be sure that the King truly is Somerset's prisoner. Were I to lead a body of armed men against the security of Windsor Palace, it could be seen as an act of treason — perhaps a further attack on the King's life. That is how Somerset would describe it to Edward, and my next residence would be the Tower.'

'Then what do you suggest?' Richard asked, thoroughly out of his depth in current matters of Court intrigue.

'We need a way of discovering the true state of things inside the royal apartments,' Dudley explained, 'and you have of course come ready supplied with our spy, in the person of your charming daughter. She is expected at Windsor, in order to join her lifelong companion Lady Jane, so there will be no suspicion raised when she is escorted thither by either yourself or myself, in either case with a suitable escort. The question that occupies my head at present is how she may thereafter send us news of the true state of things behind the ring of Somerset's men.'

Richard turned to Grace. 'That young suitor of yours — "Allan" — he is still here at Durham House?'

'Do you mean Allan Bestwick?' Dudley asked.

Guildford turned to Richard Ashton. 'Allan is my father's squire and my lifelong companion, just as Grace has been to Jane.'

'So if Grace is installed inside the royal apartments, seemingly as a mere companion to Jane, Allan could visit her in the guise of her ardent suitor?' Richard asked.

'I cannot think of any role he would rather play,' Guildford said, 'and there would be no "guise" about it.'

Richard turned to Grace. 'And I would imagine that you would have no objection to regular visits from your young man?'

'Of course not.' Grace grinned broadly.

Richard looked back at Dudley. 'What do you think?'

Dudley beamed back at him. 'We would seem to have the matter resolved.'

The two girls danced up and down with delight as they were reunited under the benevolent smile of King Edward. Grace's entry into the Audience Chamber had been announced by an usher and she had not even noticed the slender young man in the throne seat to one side as she caught sight of Jane and rushed towards her with a gleeful shout. As Jane disentangled herself from Grace's embrace, she nodded towards the King.

'Say hello to Edward — he's heard so much about you!'

Grace's smile disappeared instantly as the realisation dawned. 'You mean *King* Edward?'

'Who else?' Edward said. 'Welcome to Windsor Palace, Mistress Ashton.'

'I'm so sorry, please forgive me!'

'For what? Making my dear Jane so happy?'

'For my ignoring you and not curtseying or something, I meant.'

'Jane has not curtsied since the first time we met, and neither should you. We are all friends, I hope, so come and sit with us and enjoy some wine.'

'Did you get my latest letter?' Jane asked eagerly.

Grace nodded. 'I am sent to enquire whether or not you are really imprisoned.'

'Sent by whom?' Edward asked.

'By my father and Sir John Dudley, Duke of Northumberland.'

'And if we are, is he in a position to secure our release?'

'Yes, Your ... Your ... what should I call you?'

'Edward,' the King laughed. 'Your very clever friend here obviously achieved her purpose and yes, we are indeed not free to leave the confines of the Lower Ward — certainly not beyond its gates — so you could say that we are imprisoned.'

'But you're the King,' Grace objected, earning another laugh from Edward.

'And of what value is a king, if he be not allowed to rule his country?'

'So Somerset really has you confined, as we feared?' she asked.

Edward made a rude noise before replying. 'One uncle allegedly sought to take my life and the other seeks to rule the country while holding me down as securely as if I were in the Tower. Those guards you saw outside the chamber serve Somerset and are no doubt being richly rewarded for their treason.'

'So you wish Dudley to be informed, so that he may secure your release?'

Edward frowned. 'Would that this could occur, but you'll be saddened to hear that you are now as confined in here as we have been these past few months. How do you propose to get word to Dudley?'

'Through his squire, I hope,' Grace replied nervously. 'He and I are ... well...'

'They're in love,' Jane told Edward with a knowing smile.

'We are certainly very close,' Grace confirmed, 'and the plan is for him to visit me as my suitor and then take back word to his master that he is to bring a force to release you.'

'And how will he get past the guards?' Edward asked, unconvinced.

'That I do not know,' Grace conceded, 'but I have every faith in him.'

Three days later, Allan gained entry into the Lower Ward, past two sets of guards, dressed in the livery of the Duke of Northumberland, by the simplest ruse he could think of.

'Yer not one of us,' he was told by the senior guard on the outer gate.

'I'm a soldier, aren't I?' Allan replied, 'and I'm here at the invitation of one of the kitchen girls, who I met down in the King's Arms the other night.'

'Which one?' the guard demanded.

Allan feigned a look of uncertainty before replying, 'She said her name was "Amy", but to tell you the honest truth, we didn't go in for a lot of talking.'

'And where was yer plannin' on meetin' 'er?'

'In the kitchen, where else?' Allan replied. 'But she's got her own room near the stables, or so she assured me. Have I been misled?'

'Prob'ly not,' the guard replied. 'There's a kitchen 'and called Amy, right enough, but she looks old enough ter be yer mother. But if yer likes 'em a bit ripe, then that's yer own business. Just tell 'er that if she likes a bit of a roll durin' 'er off duty hours, Jack at the front gate's always 'appy ter oblige. You'll find the kitchen on the ground floor o' the Curfew Tower.'

'I'll make sure to pass on your message,' Allan assured him as he walked through the gate. Then it was through to the second set of guards, at the entrance to the Curfew Tower, with a new ruse unsuspectingly supplied by the Lower Ward gate guard.

'Jack at the front gate sent me through with a message for Amy in the kitchen,' Allan told the two men who barred his passage with crossed halberds.

One of them grinned. 'Dirty bastard's setting 'imself up fer a fuck, is 'e?'

'No idea,' Allan replied. 'I'm new around here.'

'That explains yer livery,' the guard replied. 'Northumberland, ain't it?'

'Yeah, but I quit that shower of pansies,' Allan told him as he spat heartily towards the ground at his feet. 'As soon as the armourer gets off his arse, I'll be in Somerset colours, like the rest of you.'

'On yer go through,' the guard agreed as he and his companion stepped sideways to allow Allan's passage between them.

This is too easy, Allan chuckled to himself as he made his way inside the Curfew Tower and enquired after the location of the laundry. Two minutes later he'd found a laundress called Bess and employed his most persuasive boyish charm as he enquired of her if she had any laundry for delivery to the Lady Jane.

'I've got a couple of 'er shifts,' Bess replied with a grin, 'but I don't reckon they'd fit you.'

'I wasn't seeking to wear them,' Allan replied, 'but I am seeking an excuse to visit her companion, or lady-in-waiting, depending on how she titles herself. Her name's "Grace" and she and I have an arrangement.'

'I dread ter think what about,' Bess leered back, 'but if yer ever get tired o' young girls, there's many a good time ter be 'ad wi' older women like me. I could teach yer lots, my lad, believe me.'

'I believe you.' Allan grinned as he made a show of gazing down the front of her loose-fitting bodice at the mounds of freckled bosom that it housed. 'Maybe when I get back from visiting Grace, which I can't do without an excuse. So those shifts, if you'd be so good?'

During his hasty walk down the main hallway with two highly decorated ladies' shifts over his arm Allan attracted a few catcalls from guards dressed in the Somerset livery and at least one wolf whistle. Finally he reached the doors to the Audience Chamber, where two more crossed halberds blocked his path and an usher enquired as to his business.

'I'm delivering these garments to the Lady Jane,' he announced.

'I didn't think they were yours,' the usher replied sarcastically, 'but why are you delivering them here, and why isn't the laundress doing it?'

'If you mean Bess, she's still recovering from my visit,' Allan leered, 'and she's late with this delivery, or so she assured me when I got off her, so instead of my usual payment I offered to deliver them personally.'

'What's your livery?' the usher asked suspiciously.

'Northumberland,' Allan replied. 'The Duke brought me here last summer, when he was inspecting the Tower guard who were in special training and that's how I met Bess.'

'Lucky bastard,' the usher replied. 'Put in a good word for me, would you? It would improve my standing around here to go to it with a laundress.'

'Let me in there, so that I can deliver this laundry and I'll see what I can arrange,' Allan lied and two seconds later the doors were opened for him, revealing a group of three seated at the far end of the chamber.

Grace uttered a light scream of delight and rushed down the chamber to throw herself at Allan, who swung her round and round as she peppered his face with kisses.

'Never was a laundry hand so welcomed into the royal presence,' Edward chuckled.

Allan handed the shifts to Grace, explaining that they were Jane's, then continued down the chamber and bowed, before dropping one knee to the floor. 'Your Majesty,' he said in acknowledgment before Edward gestured for him to rise.

'In the present company I'm Edward,' he told Allan. 'I assume that Grace and yourself are no strangers to each other?'

'Indeed not — Edward,' Allan replied self-consciously, 'but I am here to enquire as to whether or not you require to be rescued.'

'How did you get past my gaolers?' Edward asked.

Allan smiled. 'I was obliged to tell a few lies, regrettably. The guards on Lower Ward duty believe that I am going to it with a kitchen wench called "Amy", while your usher outside believes that the object of my lust is the lady who supplied me with that laundry.'

'Excellent!' Edward enthused with a light clap of the hands.

'I hope they were lies,' Grace muttered.

'And I hope that you are here to advise us that we shall soon be free to leave here,' Edward added with a smile.

Allan nodded. 'My master simply needed confirmation that you were indeed being held against your will by Somerset and that if he approached Windsor with a large host he could not be accused of a treasonous threat against your life.'

'Your master being Northumberland?' Edward asked. 'If so, then he must have many armed men at his command. But you have my authority to bring the Yeoman Warders from the Tower as well. And before they venture west, they may secure the person of the alleged Lord Protector Somerset and place him in irons.'

'It shall be done, Your ... Edward,' Allan confirmed as he rose from his seat, bowed and began to walk down the chamber towards the door. Just before he reached it, Edward smiled at Grace by his side and nodded towards the retreating figure of their rescuer. 'The least you can do is to wish him God speed, Grace.'

Grace needed no further persuasion and raced down the carpet towards the door, calling for Allan to wait for her. As the doors closed behind them and they stood facing each other in the hallway, Grace made a grab for him and she kissed him passionately.

'Who needs a laundry woman, when that's on offer?' the usher muttered to himself.

XXI

Two evenings later, as the sun began setting over distant Reading, the lookout on the main gate recently constructed by the late King Henry shouted down that a large host was approaching. The maximum available guard was called out, including those officially off duty and as Sir John Dudley and his son Guildford commanded their mounts to a halt before the closed gates, over a hundred of Somerset's force glared down at them from the south walls.

'I come on the authority of His Majesty the King!' Dudley bellowed up at them. 'Open the gates, by royal command!'

'We take our orders from the Lord Protector!' came the reply from the Captain of the Guard.

'There is no Lord Protector, since the early hours of this morning!' Dudley yelled back. 'He is currently in the Tower, accused of treason, as my son here can confirm, since it was he who conducted him thither. If you do not believe me, address yourself to the Constable of the Tower, who rides immediately behind me with his own force and with instructions to arrest all who resist our entry. There are three thousand of us in total, whereas you can probably field no more than two hundred. Yield now and be adjudged loyal, or resist our entry and be hung, drawn and quartered as traitors. The choice is yours, but I am impatient for my supper.'

After only the briefest of delays, the gates ground open and Dudley led the first few ranks of his horse-drawn force into the Lower Ward, then turned in the saddle and called for Allan Bestwick. 'Where to now?' he asked.

'The Curfew Tower, up ahead,' Allan nodded. 'The first floor hallway contains the Audience Chamber.'

Dudley smiled. 'You have waited over-long for your knighthood, Allan, but now by way of reward you may lead the force that liberates the King from his bondage. You have earned that, at least.'

Ten minutes later, Edward, Grace and Jane looked up in eager anticipation as the Audience Chamber door was kicked in and in strolled Allan Bestwick at the head of a group of serious looking men-at-arms wielding large swords. The rest of the company held back as Allan strolled the full length of the chamber, then bowed and knelt.

'You are no longer detained, Your Majesty, and my men and I await your further instruction.'

'You have led this army yourself?' Edward asked. 'Where is Northumberland?'

'Behind me, sire, with his son and the rest of the force. It was his command that I lead this final party into the Curfew Tower. They are below, I believe.'

'Guildford!' Jane called as she left her seat and raced past Allan and out of the chamber.

As Allan turned to follow with his eyes her somewhat unorthodox departure from the royal presence, Edward turned to Grace with a smile. 'Time to welcome back your hero.'

A few moments later the group of armed men in the chamber doorway parted to reveal the entry of Sir John Dudley, Guildford by his side and Jane hanging on Guildford's arm as if determined never to release it.

Sir John smiled at the sight of Grace wrapped around Allan, before executing a bow towards Edward. 'I believe that our arrival is neither unexpected nor unwelcome.'

Edward leapt to his feet. 'Indeed not, and my undying thanks for your timely arrival. We tired of Windsor some weeks ago and now, if we may, we'd like to return to Greenwich.'

'With your permission,' Dudley replied, 'I believe that Grace will wish to return to Durham House, where her father awaits our safe return. It was he who alerted us to your plight and no doubt he will wish to take her back to the comfort of his estate in Leicestershire.'

'Tell me more about him,' Edward requested as he waved his hand in Grace's direction. 'He has clearly raised a most resourceful daughter.'

'He is Sir Richard Ashton, Your Majesty, and he was formerly in the service of Master Secretary Thomas Cromwell, until Cromwell was executed for reasons that still remain obscure and Sir Richard fell under threat from Norfolk. But since the latter is still in the Tower, along now with Seymour, Sir Richard felt emboldened to return to London in order to secure your release.'

'But he did not ride here as one of your company?'

'No, Your Majesty, since he is no soldier.'

'Talking of the Tower, may I instruct you to collect Wriothesley from wherever he is currently skulking and convey him there also?' Edward asked. 'Despite being told that his commission was at an end, he took it upon himself to ask impertinent questions of the Lady Jane.'

'You will not have heard,' Dudley replied with a smile, 'since you have been kept isolated here these past few weeks. Wriothesley died two weeks past — some say of a broken heart, that he was unable to fulfil his mission, but others speak of poison.'

'Perhaps he swallowed one of his own reports,' Edward said, 'but we are well rid of him, whatever the cause of his demise.

153

We shall perhaps never know who was behind Baron Seymour's plot against my life.'

'There is a popular belief that whoever put him up to it was intent on bringing him down,' Dudley observed. 'Given recent events, perhaps he was ill advised by his older brother.'

Edward seemed lost in thought for a moment, then he looked directly up at Dudley. 'Since that older brother is now my guest in the Tower, it would seem that my Council is in need of a new leader. You would seem to be Somerset's most likely successor as Lord Protector, if you would accept the role.'

Dudley bowed in appreciation. 'I would gladly be of further service to in the matter of convening the Council, Your Majesty, but if you would accept my respectful counsel in the spirit in which it is intended, you should now take the leadership of it yourself. You are less than four years from taking the entire burdens of State upon your own shoulders and in that limited time it would be of inestimable assistance to you were you to guide the Council in those policies that you deem appropriate.'

'You wish me to govern the country alone?' Edward asked with a look of horror. 'I have neither the knowledge nor the experience. You must help me in this, Dudley.'

Sir John smiled. 'Gladly, sire, but not in the manner that led Somerset to his downfall. He grew arrogant under the temptation of his almost absolute power. No man should ever be placed in that position again, so with your gracious leave I will accept the role of "Lord President of Council", in which capacity I will assist in the selection of other Council members, but will only be empowered to act upon the decision of the majority, countersigned with your consent. There is much work to be done in the restoration of this troubled realm and it is paramount that you be seen to be in the forefront of improvements in trade, commerce, foreign policy and of course our national religion.'

'So I must spend more time in Council and less time with Lady Jane? What say you to this, Jane?'

Jane blushed slightly and her eyes fell to the carpet as she mumbled: 'You are the King, Edward, and Sir John is right to request that you lend your wisdom to the governance of your kingdom until such time as the Council is no longer required. But, should you so desire, I will make my residence in London and will attend upon you whenever you summon me.'

'I would seem to have no choice,' Edward conceded with a smile. 'But will your father not require you on his estate?'

'I have two sisters, Edward, and my father has ever been more attentive to the next oldest, Catherine. My absences from his estate have grown so frequent and so lengthy, of late, that I do not believe he would grieve unduly were I to transfer my residence to the city.'

'You were previously resident with the Dudleys, were you not?'

'Indeed I was, and happily so.'

'Dudley?' Edward asked in a tone of voice that was both a prompt and a command.

Dudley bowed. 'It would be both a privilege and a pleasure to welcome her back into my extensive household, sire.'

'What about me?' Grace piped up without thinking, then placed an instinctive hand over her mouth as she realised her presumption. It was Jane who saved her from further embarrassment.

'Indeed, Edward. Grace has ever been my companion and I would that she be allowed to remain with me. If Sir John would graciously consent...'

'Of course he would,' Edward insisted, adding, 'Wouldn't you, my Lord President of Council?'

'Naturally, Your Majesty,' Dudley conceded with another bow. 'Apart from any other consideration, the presence of Grace Ashton in my household will guarantee the continued presence of a squire who might otherwise seek another master in his incessant ambition for a knightly title.'

'But we must of course obtain your father's consent to your transfer down here,' Edward insisted.

Grace grinned. 'You may leave my father to me, Edward.'

Edward was led back in regal splendour to his favoured Greenwich Palace, with much blowing of horns and the cheering of crowds that had been whipped up to line the streets in advance by a company of men led by Guildford and Allan. Then Dudley took his leave and returned to Durham House with the small group of Guildford, Allan, Jane and Grace, in order to reassure the waiting Richard Ashton that their mission had been accomplished without loss of blood, and that King Edward had asked that his grateful thanks be passed on to his loyal subject, Sir Richard.

While Richard was still glowing with this recognition, Dudley took his opportunity.

'His Majesty is much taken with young Grace and has requested that she be allowed to remain here at Durham House, as the companion to Jane that she has ever been. It is a wonderful opportunity for her to meet likely marriage partners among the many ennobled visitors who grace this establishment, as well as those who frequent the Court.'

Richard smiled politely, but looked unconvinced. 'It was ever my ambition to preserve Grace from the intrigue, back-stabbing and betrayal that besmirched the Court during my day, and indeed led to the demise of her birth mother. She no doubt willingly agreed to remain, since she finds life at Knighton too restrictive of her inquisitive nature, but she is a mere thirteen years old and lacks judgment. Before I give my consent, I would wish to speak, not only with her, but also with that excellent young man who seems to have engaged her heart.'

'Allan Bestwick?' Dudley asked disparagingly. 'He is a mere squire in my service.'

'I was once lower even than that,' Richard replied with a smile, 'until Cromwell found me on the country estate in which I would have withered and died in obscurity.'

'But he lifted you high at Court, did he not? And are the rumours true that among your ancestors may be listed former members of the royal House of York?'

Richard paled and reached out to touch Dudley's sleeve. 'No more on that, I beg you. It proved to be more of a curse than a blessing, and it is one of the reasons why I would not wish my daughter's true heritage to be generally known. Norfolk may be in the Tower, but he still commands powerful followers.'

'As you wish. Wait here a moment, while I bring Grace and Allan to your side.'

'You will no doubt find them together,' Richard said.

Five minutes later, Grace was on the point of persuading her father, in the much-practised manner that he could no more resist on this occasion than on the previous ones, when Richard turned to Allan with a hard stare.

'One would need to be blind not to notice that you have captured Grace's heart. Once, when a small girl, she innocently announced, to my horror, that if anyone offended her, she would get her husband to "run him through". Rest assured, Master Bestwick, that should you wrong my daughter in any way — and, I emphasise, *in any way* — then I shall lose not a moment in running you through. Are we understood?'

'Perfectly, sir, and my love for Grace is such that your sword arm will never be troubled on my account.'

'Then I place my dearest daughter in your sole care, Master Bestwick, and ask only that you do not wed her anywhere but in the presence of myself and the woman she has always regarded as her mother.'

'We have not yet spoken of marriage, Father,' Grace told him with a slightly red face.

'Then the sooner you begin that conversation, the better,' Richard replied, before pulling Grace towards him and wishing her every good fortune with a voice cracking with emotion.

It was obvious at the very first Council meeting following King Edward's return to Greenwich that matters would be conducted very differently under the Duke of Northumberland. The most immediately obvious change was the fact that King Edward not only attended in person but took an active part in the discussions on every issue, ranging from England's ongoing relationship with France to the preservation of law and order throughout the nation.

There was an urgent need to reduce military expenditure in all previous arenas and one of Dudley's more controversial successes was to persuade Council of the need to sign a peace treaty with France that permitted the withdrawal of English forces from Boulogne. At about the same time, Dudley began sending out envoys into mainland Europe to seek a politically appropriate bride for Edward, settling eventually on the six-year-old Elizabeth of Valois, daughter of King Henry II of France, and close friend of Mary of Scotland.

But although the new regime appeared on its surface to be less dictatorial than the old system under Somerset, in reality Dudley had more control over the affairs of the nation than even his predecessor. He made sure that the Council members who were appointed — notionally by the young King — were all sympathetic to him and grateful for their elevation. Men such as Sir John Gates and Lord Thomas Darcy were content to follow Dudley's lead and he even contrived to place his son-in-law Sir Henry Sidney and his brother Sir Andrew Dudley close to the King in a newly constituted 'Counsel for the Estate', which effectively ran the royal household.

But Dudley did not get everything his own way. In a fit of magnanimity that blew up in his face, Dudley persuaded King Edward to release his uncle from the Tower and restore him to the Council. This was a short-lived initiative, since Seymour was discovered to be plotting his old rival's downfall and was executed.

There was also some nervous murmuring against the extent of the religious reforms that were being pushed through at King Edward's insistence. He had taken wholeheartedly to the Reformist initiative inside the realm and even Archbishop Cranmer was heard to express his unease at the speed with which reforms such as the rejection of the doctrine of transubstantiation, the proclamation of 'justification by faith' and the denial of the existence of Purgatory were pushed through Council at the insistence of the young King.

This did nothing for his relationship with his older sister, Mary, who sullenly refused to acknowledge any of it and had all but converted her country residence at Hunsdon into a Roman Catholic shrine at which all those of what she perceived to be the 'true faith' might come and worship. When she was ordered by Edward, through the hand of Dudley, to moderate her stance, she blankly refused and noisily threatened to flee the country for Spain, even instructing the Imperial Ambassador de Scheyfye to declare war on England.

Nothing came of the threat of war, after the Ambassador was bluntly advised by Dudley that the Lady Mary was courting her own doom by issuing such challenges to the realities at Court. In the midst of all this, Elizabeth sat quietly at home in Hatfield, watching the verbal missiles flying over her head but saying nothing.

XXII

The first indication of the forthcoming storm in the Tudor dynastic ocean was the message brought to Dudley, ahead of the scheduled weekly meeting of Council, that King Edward would not be in attendance because he had a heavy cold. Since it was mid-January there was felt to be no cause for concern and given that there was nothing particularly contentious on the Council agenda for that day, Dudley was able to steer the Council into decisions that he and Edward had already discussed in advance.

Two weeks — and two more missed Council meetings later — the heavy cold had become a fever and a persistent cough, and Dudley sought more detailed advice from one of the royal physicians, who shook his head in a gesture of uncertainty and did his best to explain in terms that an ordinary listener would understand.

'In truth, his constitution has been weak these two years past, following those recurrent bouts of sweating sickness that assailed him as a mere child. He has a weakness of the chest that is provoked whenever he catches even a common cold, and in previous days he has complained of a difficulty in drawing breath, due, so far as can be divined, from a constriction of the internal organs on his right side.'

'And your prognosis?'

'I am a physician, my Lord, not a soothsayer. His constitution is weak, as I already said and even if he survives this latest challenge to his health, there will be others. It is as well that the nation is so well governed by Council when the King is thus indisposed.'

Edward's condition seemed to improve with the advent of spring, and in early April he made a point of walking through the royal gardens at Westminster Palace arm in arm with Jane, with various members of his household in attendance, in order to dispel rumours that were circulating through the city that his days were numbered and that the Lady Mary was busy organising a move south from her country hermitage in Hertfordshire to impose 'the old ways' back upon the Church.

Dudley had read the warning signs, however, and lost no time on calling in at Lambeth Palace, the official residence of Archbishop Thomas Cranmer when in London, and only a short wherry trip across the river from the Palace of Westminster.

'Forgive my intrusion into your personal life, Thomas,' Dudley began, by way of a veiled reference to Cranmer's wife, the German-born Margarete and their two children, all hidden away in Kent, but silently tolerated for as long as Cranmer was of use to the Reform movement. 'I wish you to advise me further on a matter to which you made reference when King Edward lay on what he believed to be his deathbed some time ago now.'

'The matter of the succession?' Cranmer asked with a nod. 'I have been giving great thought to it myself in recent weeks, but, God be praised, it seems that the King is back to his own again.'

'Has he changed his will since that time?' Dudley asked eagerly.

Cranmer shook his head. 'Not in my presence, anyway.'

'And he still confides in you?'

'Indeed.'

'So if Edward were to die, the direct succession would go to Jane Grey?'

'As I understand it. The document still lies in Chancery, should you wish to read it for yourself.'

'No, your word is sufficient, as indeed is your memory. It was once our belief — well, mine anyway — that Edward would make Jane his bride, but it would seem that now he is to be betrothed to Valois, his only remaining way of declaiming to the world the affection he bears toward Jane is to leave her England.'

'You forget his piety and good grace,' Cranmer reminded him. 'He is tortured by the thought that all that he has striven for in the retreat from Rome will be lost should the crown go to Mary.'

'I suspect that we shall all be lost should Mary become Queen, Thomas. And so I bid you good day.'

Back home, Dudley called for Guildford to attend upon him, poured them both two generous mugs of wine and wasted no further time in idle chit-chat.

'Dudley, what think you of the Lady Jane?'

There was an embarrassed silence, broken eventually by a red-faced Guildford. 'Has Mistress Calthorpe been telling tales?'

'What tales would they be?' Dudley asked.

'That Mistress Jane and I walk in the garden most days, as companions to Mistress Grace and Allan, mainly to ensure that they don't go to it under the cherry blossom when Mistress Calthorpe falls asleep.'

'And yourself and Jane? You are not minded to go to it?'

'Father!' Guildford protested, red-faced, but Dudley merely tutted.

'I shall clearly have to speak more directly. Were I to order you to wed the Lady Jane, you would have no objection?'

Guildford's eyes widened and his mouth broke into a joyful smile. 'I would regard it as a happy privilege. But I do not know if she would have me, were I to put the question to her.'

'You will not be doing that — I will, once I have persuaded her father,' Dudley told him.

'Is that not my part?' Guildford asked.

Dudley shook his head. 'Not on this occasion. Do you simply prepare yourself to go along with what your loving and supportive father has in mind.'

Two evenings later, the Greys were invited to supper with the Dudleys, on the pretext of discussing some matters of State that were due for debate in Council that week. Because of their confidential nature the young people of the household had taken supper earlier and were now to be heard in an upper chamber, laughing and affectionately disputing over a game of shuffleboard.

Dudley sat back in his chair, wine goblet in hand, with his wife Jane by his side and smiled at Henry and Frances Grey. 'Our son and your daughter seem to be well matched, do they not?'

'Indeed,' Henry Grey confirmed with a smile of his own, 'we are gratified that she has such fitting companions here in London, which we know from our own experience can be a lonely and hazardous place. Thank you also for accommodating her lifelong friend Grace Ashton, without whom she would perhaps feel a little lost.'

Dudley smiled even more widely. 'Mistress Grace needs little encouragement to remain here on her own account, since she is greatly enamoured of my own squire, Allan Bestwick. The four of them make a happy sight here at Durham House, forever in each other's company. For an old man like me, it is a reminder of my more romantic days.'

'Are you saying that our daughter Jane and your son Guildford may be becoming romantically inclined towards each other?' Frances Grey asked.

Dudley nodded. 'Indeed they are, which is one of the matters I wished to discuss with you this evening. Guildford has confessed to me his growing affection for your daughter and I thought it only appropriate to advise you of this, since should it not meet with your approval I could arrange to nip it in the bud — perhaps by sending Guildford abroad to fight in our next war across the Channel.'

'You would expose your son to the prospect of death in order to protect our daughter from unwanted advances?' Henry Grey asked admiringly.

His wife was more guarded. 'His Lordship did not say that such advances were unwanted, Henry.' She smiled at Dudley before continuing. 'Have you by any chance enquired of Jane whether or not she would accept Guildford's suit?'

'Not as yet, no,' Dudley conceded. 'But I watch them when they are together and it seems to me that there is much more affection between them than can be observed in many arranged marriages these days.'

'You are proposing such a match between our offspring?' Henry Grey asked.

'Assuming that there is love between them, would you object to such? I am well aware that Jane is barely fifteen years old, but she presents, in both mind and body, as much older than that.'

Henry and Frances Grey exchanged excited looks and nodded to each other. It was left to Henry to express their consent.

'You would be correct to believe that Jane is very special to us, as our first-born, and she promises much more than our second daughter, Catherine, and our youngest, Mary, who to some tastes would even be regarded as plain. But Jane has proved to be engaging enough even for the young man who is now King; indeed there was a time when we were led to believe that he might think of her as a bride for himself. But now that he is spoken for to a princess of France, what could be more fitting that Jane should marry into the highest ennobled family in the land, short of the Tudor household itself? So yes, you honour us with the suggestion that our families should be joined in this way.'

Dudley raised his wine goblet in the air, in the gesture of a toast. 'And we would of course rejoice to see our son happily joined in matrimony with so gracious a young lady. With your agreement, we would wish the happy event to be organised with little delay. And perhaps we could make it a joint occasion.'

'In what way?' Frances asked.

'You mentioned a second daughter — "Catherine", I believe you said her name was. A girl of twelve, according to what Jane tells us?'

'That's correct,' Henry Grey confirmed, 'but what of her?'

'Forgive my presumption,' Dudley oozed, 'but only some days ago I was speaking with my fellow Councillor, the Earl of Pembroke, brother-in-law of the late Queen Catherine, through his marriage to her sister Anne. He is seeking a bride for his heir, Henry, who will in due course inherit the Pembroke title and I undertook to enquire as to suitable young ladies of appropriate lineage to grace such a title, one of the most respected in the realm.'

'Twelve is a little young,' Frances observed reluctantly, until her husband reached for her hand and kissed it.

'So is fifteen and yet we have just consented to Jane's betrothal and early marriage. And I remember a shy sixteen-year-old who once stood by my side at your father's house at Suffolk Place and pledged her life to me in a gesture I have always regarded as the greatest gift that God ever bestowed on me.'

Frances blushed and looked back at Dudley. 'So, a double wedding, perhaps?'

'Make that triple,' Dudley replied. 'We have a daughter, Katherine, who is the same age as your Jane and she has been asked for in marriage to Henry Hastings, the heir to the Earldom of Huntingdon. We have yet to give consent, but given the happy miasma of young love that has wreathed itself around us this evening, I speak also for my wife when I say that we would be overjoyed for this house to be the scene of six young people entering into a lifelong adventure which for Jane and I has been a voyage of joy. Let us raise our hands in a toast ahead of advising the happy couples.'

XXIII

'You'd have expected Allan to propose to me, in the spirit of all the other weddings that are being planned,' Grace complained as she dressed Jane's hair for the final time, an hour before the ceremony.

Although it was a happy day for Jane, she felt deep sympathy for her lifelong friend. 'Has he said nothing?' she asked.

Grace shook her head. 'Only the usual nonsense about waiting until he has his knighthood and his estate, neither of which is likely to be happening soon, I suspect. Will your new father-in-law be granting you an estate?'

'Perhaps,' Jane replied absent-mindedly as she gazed carefully into the hand mirror held up for her by Grace, scrutinising both her face and the red hair peeking out from under the French hood. 'Should I be showing that much hair?' she asked.

'I have no idea,' Grace replied sourly, 'since I have no experience of Courtly fashion — unlike some girls who once rolled in the Leicestershire mud.'

Jane was able to put Grace's surly discontent out of her mind during the splendid triple wedding ceremony in the Great Hall of Durham House, conducted by Archbishop Cranmer as a special favour to the President of Council John Dudley, who had always acted in his best interests and therefore the best interests of the Protestant faith in England.

Once all the couples had been put to bed in the Tudor style in the specially provisioned bedchambers on the upper floors, John Dudley wandered out into the balmy air of the late spring night. He spotted movement further down the lawn and strolled down to join the Archbishop.

'My grateful thanks once again, Thomas, for your service today.'

'As a personal thanks to you, it was the least I could offer,' Cranmer replied. 'I just hope that Guildford and Jane enjoy a long and happy life together.'

'Why might they not?' Dudley asked.

Cranmer looked sideways at him with a cynical smile. 'Your son did not marry simply a daughter of the Greys, or even a daughter of Suffolk, as of course you were aware, thanks to me. If Edward dies without revoking his will, Jane will be Queen of England. No doubt this match was of your making in that knowledge. I'm not sure of the protocols, but do you see Guildford as King?'

'That will clearly be a matter for Council,' Dudley replied. 'But what ground have you for believing that King Edward will soon be a memory?'

'From what his physicians advise me daily,' Cranmer replied, 'His Majesty staggers from one ailment to another. He was well enough to display himself to the people a few weeks since and has since made great show of appearing on occasions at his chamber window to watch the ships on the river. But then he fell back into a lengthy coughing fit in which he is said to have spewed up blood. And when was he last present at Council?'

'He trusts me to make known his wishes when we meet,' Dudley replied evasively.

Cranmer shook his head sadly. 'Which makes you no better than Somerset was, at the height of his power. Take care that you do not over-reach yourself, my Lord, because those of us who are bringing the true faith back to the people rely upon you for our protection. Should Edward die and should we proclaim Jane as Queen in order to preserve that true faith, what would be the likely response of the Lady Mary?'

'We will, as they are wont to say, cross that bridge when we come to it, Thomas. Now, no more of this gloom. Come back inside with me and let us partake of some more wine.'

Three days later, King Edward attended his last Council meeting, held at Greenwich for his convenience, but he was obliged to leave towards the end, when a fit of coughing left him bent double over the table, with a residue of pinkish froth the only reminder that he had been there. He was carried back to his bedchamber, where he lay for several days, complaining of a swelling in his legs and an inability to breathe. Among those who were allowed to attend upon him was Archbishop Cranmer, and during his first audience Edward grabbed his wrist with a bony but insistent hand.

'Have we really pursued the true faith, my Lord Archbishop, or am I destined for Hell?'

'The faith we have promoted has been God's gift to the nation, Your Majesty,' Cranmer assured him, 'and by its promotion you have assured your seat in Heaven. But not yet, you will see — this temporary affliction will soon be past and you will once again be able to show yourself to your adoring subjects who gather daily under your window for sight of you.'

'You have preserved my will? The one I made some time past?'

'Of course, Your Majesty. It is being held in Chancery, as you commanded.'

'And is ought else required to make it law?'

'It requires to be converted into letters patent, which must be signed by Council, the bishops and the judges of the Kings Bench.'

'See to it, my Lord Archbishop, and have Jane Grey attend me once it has been prepared for patenting.'

Three days later, Jane sat tearfully by Edward's bed, holding his hand as his eyes opened and he smiled. 'Dearest Jane, I have made arrangements for you to be Queen.'

'I do not wish to be Queen, Edward — I simply wish for you to be well again, so that we can continue our conversations.'

'Continue to promote the true faith,' Edward urged her, ignoring her protestation. 'And pray for my soul, in case we were both wrong.'

Edward laboured on for another week, his only attendants being physicians and Cranmer. Council was summoned in order to sign the letters patent and there was soon not a worthy left in London who was not aware of the true nature of the declared succession. Word was carried to the Ladies Elizabeth and Mary that their brother was dying and Elizabeth managed a short visit, during the whole of which Edward lay coldly rasping in his unconsciousness and she was led gently from his deathbed in floods of genuine tears.

Mary's reaction was characteristically different. When advised, by the same messenger, of both Edward's impending death and his gift of the crown to Jane Grey, her steward looked at her enquiringly.

'Shall I prepare the household for travel to London, my Lady?'

Mary's face set in a stern and determined glare as she looked out through her chamber window at the gardens in full bloom. 'Prepare for travel, certainly. But we go not to London. Rather, we head to the north and east, to Norfolk, where there are those who would support me in their thousands. This upstart daughter of Grey's shall find that the crown of England sits unsteadily on her head.'

XXIV

King Edward breathed his last on 6th July, but those huddled around his deathbed, who included Dudley, needed time to discuss their next move, given their knowledge of the contents of Edward's will. They suppressed news of his death for four days and did not even tell Jane until the third day, by which time Dudley was cursing his lack of foresight in not securing Mary's person ahead of the royal demise. Word came to him that she had retreated to Framlingham Castle in Suffolk, formerly a stronghold of the Howard family until Thomas Howard had been consigned to the Tower by the now deceased Edward and the castle had been gifted to Mary. But she was among friends in East Anglia, the scene of more than one rebellion against Protestantism and the power base of the 'old' Norfolk family.

Within days they were flooding to her cause, many of them wielding weapons retrieved from attics, some of them waving nothing more than rusting farm implements, but all of them convinced that God was on Mary's side. Within two weeks of her half brother's death, Mary's force was almost twenty thousand strong.

From the safety of the Norfolk family seat at Kenninghall, Mary fired off a despatch to the Council, demanding that she be proclaimed as Queen. Dudley had anticipated this and the day before her demand arrived he had Jane escorted to the safety of the royal apartments in the Tower, along with her husband of only a few weeks, Guildford. This was traditionally the residence of every incoming monarch ahead of their actual coronation and in order to leave no-one in any doubt about what was happening Dudley ordered that heralds be sent out into the London streets to proclaim Jane as Queen of England.

A stunned populace, who had expected the joyful return to London of Mary and her more familiar and comfortable Catholicism, could only gather on street corners and mutter their unease, while Jane, still protesting that she had no wish to be Queen, was advised that she must make plans for her coronation and begin selecting her household.

She found Grace sitting disconsolately on the lawn of Tower Green, her bare feet tucked demurely under her long smock, watching the birds as they cocked their heads sideways to listen for the movement of worms after the recent shower.

'There you are,' Jane announced as she stood looking down at Grace. 'I've been looking everywhere for you, since I have a favour to ask.'

'I'll hazard a guess that it's not a request to join you in rolling across the lawn here, in case you dirty your queenly robes,' Grace muttered.

Jane's heart fell to her highly decorated leather pattens. 'Dearest Grace,' Jane replied coaxingly as she squatted down to place her arm over Grace's shoulder, 'I didn't ask to be Queen, I don't want to be Queen, and I refuse to be Queen if it means that I'll be losing my best friend.'

Grace looked up at her with tear-streaked cheeks. 'I'm not out of sorts because you're Queen — I just want to know where Allan's got to. I haven't seen him since the weddings — has Sir John sent him off to fight a war somewhere?'

'I have no idea,' Jane replied, 'and Guildford's been looking for him since yesterday, in order to ask if he'd be prepared to be our Chamberlain. But the way you ignored him at the tourneys after the weddings, who could blame him for running away from you? He was seen in the stables afterwards, crying his eyes out while saddling a horse. It was well after dark, so perhaps he set off for that place he comes from in Nottinghamshire.'

'What was the favour you came out here to ask?' Grace asked.

Jane chose her words with the utmost care. 'Do you remember one time when we were walking together in Bradgate and you asked if you would still be my best friend if I became Queen of England? Remember — we both thought it was just a jest?'

'Of course I remember.'

'Well, you are still my best friend, but I want you to become my Senior Lady.'

'And what does one of those do? Run around after you, bowing and scraping?'

'Please, Grace, don't be so grumpy with me, else I'll cry, I just know I will. I may be Queen of England and married and all that, but I still need you by my side the whole time. Life somehow loses its flavour when you're not around — I learned that when we were held captive in Windsor.'

'I'll be your "Senior Lady", as you call it, if you'll do something for me,' Grace told her hopefully as she stared hard at the White Tower, shimmering after the recent rain.

'Anything,' Jane replied eagerly. 'What is it you want?'

'Nothing for myself. But for Allan — a knighthood and an estate. It need only be a small one. Then perhaps — if he ever comes back — we can — can...' Her shoulders shook.

Jane hitched up her gown and threw herself down onto the tightly scythed grass in order to fold Grace into her arms. 'Darling Grace — please don't worry! He'll come back, you'll see. And when he does, we'll make him the Earl of somewhere or other, and give him a castle with a moat and servants and a deer park, and whatever else he wants. Just don't cry like that — it breaks my heart to hear it. If you stop, we can roll across the grass together, just like we used to do.'

Grace began to giggle and her tears had been reduced to the occasional hiccup by the time that John Dudley appeared behind them with serious news.

'Mary has ordered Council to proclaim her Queen, ahead of her march down here with a force of many thousands. I've dispatched ships to the Norfolk coast, to prevent her escaping across to France or Spain, but Council have ordered me north with an army, to prevent her reaching London. Where the Hell is Allan?'

'We don't know,' Jane told him. 'We think he rode off on the evening of the weddings, but no-one's seen him since. I hope you're not going to take Guildford instead?'

'Of course not, but if Allan shows himself in the next day or so, tell him to follow us north to Cambridge.'

They watched Dudley's retreating back as he headed for the stables and Grace was puzzled.

'What made you think that Sir John could order your husband to ride with him? Isn't he the King now?'

Jane shook her head with a smile. 'He'd like to be, but until I can ask the advice of Council — my Council now, I suppose — I'm not sure how these things work. I'm told that I can make him a Duke, but not King. I don't think he believes me and he's not very happy about it.'

Guildford Dudley was not the only one who was not happy. The day after Dudley had been ordered by Council to ride north to oppose Mary's force, it met to formally consider the document that she had sent, in which she demanded her 'right and title to the throne of England bequeathed to me by my royal father', adding that anyone who opposed her lawful accession would be deemed a traitor and dealt with accordingly.

It was a nervous Council that met to consider Mary's demand. In the absence of Dudley they were meeting without their usual leader, in order to consider the gravest matter that had ever been put before them and one that had long-term implications for the nation. It also directly concerned their own necks if they were wrong.

'What's the latest news from Dudley?' the Earl of Pembroke enquired nervously, acutely conscious of the fact that his son was now married to Jane's sister and that his neck would be early on the block should Mary's forces prevail.

'Last heard of in Cambridge,' the Earl of Arundel told them. 'He's outnumbered seven to one, according to the latest despatch and Mary's army's all over East Anglia.'

'Is it possible that we got it wrong?' asked a terrified Marquess of Northampton.

There was a loud and nervous response, with everyone talking at once, until Pembroke raised a hand for silence and good order.

'We simply implemented the late King's dying wishes, did we not? The letters patent came through for our signature weeks ago.'

'But they haven't yet gone through Parliament,' Northampton replied, 'and as I understand these things, that means that they're not yet law.'

'Whether they're law or not,' the Earl of Arundel pointed out, 'Mary has the stronger force and the London mob didn't exactly jump up and down with joy when we told them that Grey's daughter was Queen.'

'If Mary takes London, what will happen to us?' Northampton asked quaveringly.

Arundel replied with a dismissive snort. 'From what I've heard of the Lady Mary and her temper, we'll all be taken to Tower Hill and hung, drawn and quartered.'

'Let's take a vote,' Pembroke suggested.

'What's the motion?' someone down the end of the table enquired.

'Take a guess,' was Pembroke's sarcastic reply. 'We have time yet to display our loyalty to the claimant with the greater force and preserve our necks. Hands up all those who want their guts cut out in front of the mob.'

Two hands were raised tentatively, only to be lowered again when the vast majority of Council glared angrily down at them.

'Carried unanimously,' Pembroke announced. 'Now, how do we convey our loyal greetings to Queen Mary?'

XXV

It was Grace's third day as Senior Lady-in-Waiting to Queen Jane and she was beginning to settle into the position and could so fully occupy her time supervising Jane's hair and laying out her gowns that Allan's memory intruded less than it had done at first. But there was now a huge disorder beyond the Tower walls, from the general direction of Thames Street; voices were being raised in joyful shouts and it sounded as if the tradesmen had adopted their traditional habit of banging their tools noisily in a sign of rejoicing.

The dining chamber door opened and a foot soldier in the knee-length red, yellow and black surcoat that denoted him as a member of the Tower's resident force of Gentlemen Yeomen Wardens stood hesitantly in the doorway.

Jane looked up languidly, then stared and whispered: 'Grace — isn't that ... you know?'

Grace looked round for long enough to give a gleeful yell and leap from her chair towards the doorway. The man-at-arms moved his halberd to one side to avoid her being seriously injured as she hurled herself at him and began an assault on all parts of his face with eager lips.

'Allan!' she screamed. 'Where have you been? I'm so sorry about how I behaved at the weddings and I've missed you so much! I love you, Allan Bestwick, and Jane's going to give you your title and an estate, so we can get married whenever you wish. Do please tell me I haven't ruined everything — please!'

Guildford looked up from the table and frowned. 'And when you've done that and put Jane's Senior Lady out of her misery,

pray explain why you're dressed like that, and why you're not in Cambridge with my father.'

'A long story for later,' Allan replied. 'And with deep regret and the greatest of reluctance I have to advise you all that there'll be plenty of time for explanations. Can you hear the mob in the streets?'

'Yes,' Jane replied, 'we were wondering what the noise was all about. Do you know?'

'Unfortunately, I do,' Allan replied with a stern face, 'and it's why I'm here. I have to escort you to new accommodation. I have several more men outside.'

'For our own safety?' Jane asked. 'Has the mob risen in rebellion?'

'In a manner of speaking,' Allan replied solemnly. 'They're actually celebrating.'

'Celebrating what, exactly?' Guildford asked.

It fell silent for a moment until Allan gave them the bad news. 'The accession of Queen Mary. Council have proclaimed her Queen.'

'But I'm the Queen,' Jane insisted,

Allan shook his head. 'Not any longer. Your father-in-law is a prisoner, having being obliged by Council to formally surrender to Mary's forces. Norfolk was released from the Beauchamp Tower a few moments ago, and I have orders to convey Guildford to the same cell.'

'Why Guildford and not me?' Jane demanded.

'Because you're deemed to be royalty, and he isn't,' Allan replied. 'I've to convey you down the path to the Lieutenant's quarters, along with Grace.'

'So Guildford and I are to be separated?' Jane asked, horror-stricken. 'We've been married for barely two months. Have pity!'

'It's Mary's pity you should be seeking,' Allan replied sadly. 'She has ordered your arrests and secure imprisonment, on charges of treason for usurping her throne.'

'And me?' Grace asked in a small voice.

'That will depend,' Allan told her as he held her tightly to him. 'This must be our last embrace before I carry out my orders. As an act of mercy, you may finish your dinner, and I will await you all outside.'

'I do this with the greatest of reluctance and with a heavy heart, my Lady,' Sir Edward Warner, Lieutenant of the Tower, told Jane as she and Grace were shown into the secure chamber in which they seemed destined to await Queen Mary's pleasure, or otherwise. 'In truth,' he added, 'I fear that I shall not be your gaoler for long, since I was appointed by your father-in-law, and he is attainted by order of the new Queen.'

'What does "attainted" mean?' Jane asked.

Warner's face went pale as he explained, 'A finding of treason without the benefit of any trial,' he murmured softly.

'And then?' Jane asked fearfully.

'Normally an execution, my Lady.'

'No!' Jane screamed as she threw herself down on the bolster in the corner that had been provided as a bed.

Grace's hand was shaking as she reached down to comfort her.

Warner tried desperately to think of something to cheer them up. 'I'm advised by Captain Bestwick that he's a friend of the family and so I've placed him in immediate charge of your supervision. He'll bring you your meals and you'll be well provided for. Only the highest-born prisoners are allowed to reside in these apartments.'

'And how many Queens have you accommodated here?'

'Several,' Warner replied.

Grace looked him hard in the face as she asked, 'Queen Anne and Queen Catherine, both married to the late King Henry?'

'Indeed, Mistress.'

'And how long were they detained here?' Jane demanded.

Warner could only reply truthfully. 'Until their executions, my Lady.'

Mary waited until she had Dudley's formal surrender, then began her triumphant progress towards London. An early halt was made at Hunsdon, where she ordered that her entire wardrobe be loaded onto wagons for transport south and that Lady Elizabeth be summoned to join her from Hatfield.

When Elizabeth was admitted to Mary's presence in the drawing room at Hunsdon she stood defiantly on the carpet a few feet away and asked, 'Must I now curtsey to the sister I always beat at tennis?'

'That depends upon how much you value your head. I have not yet forgotten your plotting with Seymour.'

Elizabeth kept a defiant expression on her face as her heart began beating faster. 'You would not execute your own sister, at a time when you wish your newly acquired loyal subjects to love you and applaud your regal mercy?'

'There is more than one way to ensure the loyalty of one's subjects, in the same way that there is only one way to worship God.'

'Fear, in both cases,' Elizabeth observed acidly.

Mary's face hardened. 'In order to minimise the time in which we are required to commune in this manner which I find distasteful, and in a strange way somewhat poisonous, let me leave you in no doubt that you are as much my subject as those usurpers who will shortly feed the crows on Tower Hill. Beginning with the most evil of them all.'

'The Lady Jane?' Elizabeth asked.

Mary shook her head. 'She was merely the innocent dupe of the real architect of the treason. I speak of her father-in-law Dudley, who will be executed as my second act as Queen. My first was the release of Norfolk, who will no doubt be more than content to preside over the trials of Jane Grey and her husband. I shall also place Cranmer on trial, then have him burned for the heretic that he is.'

'And what do you intend for me?' Elizabeth asked in a continued tone of defiance that masked her nervousness.

'A life of obedience, both to the true Church and to your rightful Queen. Fate may have made us sisters, but that has hardly made us warm friends, has it? You will meet up with me again north of London and join me in my triumphal procession into the city, giving such appearance of sisterly joy as you are capable of. You will then attend me at Court with at least the pretence of loyalty.'

'And if I choose not to?'

'I do not recall offering you any choice. When I am ordering the trial of one unwanted relative, I can, with the same expenditure of breath, make it two. Now, leave me, and prepare to depart for London.'

It was a chastened and terrified Elizabeth who called for Kat Ashley once she had reached the privacy of her own allocated chambers and could beg for the sort of comforting cuddle that she had known as a child.

XXVI

'How did you manage to become our guard?' Grace asked Allan, in the chambers in the Lieutenant's House that offered a clear view of the outer wall of the Bell Tower through the barred window.

Jane pretended to eat as she diplomatically sat with her back to them at the table, listening intently to what Allan had to tell them.

'When I left Durham House, I had no idea where to go,' Allan explained. 'I was so heartbroken at what seemed to be your rejection of me — no, don't apologise again, you've done that a thousand times already, just let me finish my story. My first thought was to go home to Attenborough, then I couldn't bear the thought that I'd never see you again, so I began to ask myself what might be the fastest way to acquire a title and an estate, and come back and claim you.'

'So you never gave up hope of me?' Grace asked eagerly.

'I eventually remembered that when we rescued you and Jane from Windsor, Sir John had made me the messenger between his force and that of the Lieutenant of the Tower. I hoped he might remember me, so I rode down here and volunteered for the King's service, as it was then. I thought that distinguished service for the King might be the swiftest means of obtaining a title and an estate, and I was very lucky. Not only did the Lieutenant remember me, but he seemed to have formed a good opinion of me as a leader of men, so he appointed me as a Captain. The Yeomen Warders are all seasoned fighters, but they lack officers, since men with that level of experience are normally gentry in their own right.'

'And were you here when we first arrived?' Grace asked.

Allan grinned. 'I certainly was. You could have knocked me over with a codfish when I saw the ceremonial procession and learned that Jane was Queen. I was assigned to duties at the animal house that day, but I was able to see the cavalcade from a distance. Then a few days ago, we were advised by the Lieutenant during our morning roster that Jane was now a prisoner, along with her husband and her Senior Lady. I could see that he wasn't very happy to be telling us that and so I took my chance and explained that I knew the Dudley family, and that you might all be happier if you were guarded by a friendly face. He seemed relieved to hear that and allocated me to my present duties. But I didn't tell him that I once served as squire to Sir John, or that you and I were ... well, you know?'

'Betrothed?' Grace asked with a seductive grin.

'I should have proposed when I had the chance,' Allan admitted.

Jane cleared her mouth of mutton and turned to address them. 'You have every chance now and I'll pretend I'm not listening. Unless, of course, you want a witness.'

'Well?' Grace asked.

'Grace Ashton, would you consent to be my wife?'

'I'd consent to ride with you through the gates of Hell, Allan Bestwick, so yes, yes, a million times, yes!'

'At least my Senior Lady will be in a better humour in future,' Jane beamed across at them. 'Now, by way of a betrothal feast, come and help me get through this mutton. It died the day after I was born, to judge by its toughness.'

Four months later, the Guildhall was crowded to capacity as the Lord Mayor Sir Thomas White, accompanied by a Commission of notables that included Thomas Howard, Duke of Norfolk and the Earls of Bath and Derby, called for order and commanded that the prisoners be brought forth. They were escorted in by a contingent drawn from the Tower and led by Allan. In the centre was 'Jane Dudley, wife of Guildford,' as she was described on the indictment for high treason that consisted of an allegation that she had 'treacherously assumed the title and power of the Queen of England.'

Guildford was arraigned alongside her, as were two of his brothers, all on the same charge of treason. Also on trial for treasonously supporting the usurpation of the crown, even though he had merely honoured the wishes of his dying monarch, was Thomas Cranmer, who was no longer regarded as the Archbishop of Canterbury, although confirmation was still awaited from Rome to remove him formally from office. It was no secret that regardless of the outcome of the treason trial, Cranmer faced a more agonising end on a funeral pyre as the penalty for his heresy, along with Hugh Latimer, King Edward's former chaplain and Nicholas Ridley, Bishop of London, who were already in the Tower awaiting their fate.

Any high drama that the eager crowd might have been anticipating was blunted somewhat by the decision by Jane and Guildford to plead guilty to the technical charge, but with a mitigating claim that they had been the innocent pawns of others and, in Jane's case, that she had simply been fulfilling the dying wish of the young Edward to whom she had been a loyal companion. They had nothing to lose by casting the primary blame on Sir John Dudley, since he had already been executed two months earlier, following his trial for treason before a judge and jury in Westminster Hall. In what may have been an attempt to mollify Queen Mary in the hope of preserving the lives of Guildford and Jane, Dudley had made a

186

great show of renouncing his Protestant faith, which he described as 'a plague that is on the realm.'

Whether swayed by Dudley's recantation, or still persuaded that Jane was the harmless dupe of others who might incite sympathy were she to be either burned at the stake or hung, drawn and quartered, Mary chose to temporarily withhold the hand of vengeance and Jane and Guildford were ordered back to the Tower to await their ultimate destiny.

News of Jane's conviction had cast a pall of misery over the London town house of the Greys, who awoke each day with the fearful apprehension of hearing that an execution date had been set. In his off-duty hours Allan Bestwick was able to visit both the Greys and the grieving Dudley widow Jane, who was lodging with them following the forfeiture of the Northumberland estates, in order to keep them assured of the ongoing health of their offspring and that Jane and Guildford were in good spirits.

One evening, during a visit to the Greys to take supper, Allan found himself face to face with Richard and Kate Ashton, who were anxious for news of Grace.

'She bides with Jane,' he was able to tell them, 'and she brings her much comfort by her very presence.'

'Is she charged with any offence?' Richard asked.

Allan shook his head. 'None of which I have been advised, sir, but she is likely to remain with Jane until her fate is finally decided by Queen Mary. I should perhaps advise you that she has graciously consented to become my wife, once all this is over.'

'It could drag on for years!' Henry Grey reminded him loudly as he joined the company in front of the fire. 'We must take steps to have her freed.'

Allan gave them all a discouraging look. 'The Tower is the most secure fortress in the realm and you can be assured, from my own experience, that it is well guarded.'

'There may be another way,' Grey suggested in a guarded tone as he beckoned them to the table in the centre of the hall. 'Although I am expelled from Council for obvious reasons, yet I remain in contact with my good friend Sir William Thomas, who is currently its Clerk. From him I learn that there is much concern over the Queen's plan to marry, in order to provide heirs so as to block the line of accession to the Lady Elizabeth. This in itself is not, of course, of any great concern, since there are several eligible Englishmen who might be persuaded, even though she is no great beauty. But she has other ambitions, in which she is being encouraged by her cousin Charles of Spain.'

'He is too old for even her, surely?' Richard objected.

Grey nodded. 'Indeed, and of course he is still married. But he has a son, Philip, who is heir apparent, not only to great tracts of Europe, but also much land in the New World that is the source of considerable wealth in the form of gold and sugar.'

'And it is being proposed that Mary marry him?'

'Not so much proposed, as insisted on, by the Imperial Ambassador, no less. The concern within Council is of England becoming simply another outpost of Spain, as the Netherlands have recently become. And, of course, that the old Church will be restored, even more rigidly than it was before the former Queen Katherine was put aside.'

'Has Council expressed these concerns to Mary herself?' Richard asked.

Grey grimaced. 'Indeed it has and her response was that she is Queen of England and mistress of her own womb and will decide who to marry for herself, regardless of the views of Council.'

'So what is being proposed?' Richard asked fearfully. 'And what is to be demanded of me?'

'Simply your silence, at the very least, or at best perhaps your sword arm and your heritage.'

Richard's response was a hollow laugh. 'I have not wielded a sword for years and I am opposed to bloodshed. As for my bloodlines, who these days has any desire to see the House of York restored to the throne?'

'The Earl of Devon, for one,' Grey told them. 'His grandmother was Princess Catherine of York, a sister of the Prince Richard who is reputed to have been your grandfather. He is now simply Edward Courtenay and a kinsman of Queen Mary, but one of her first acts as Queen was to release him from the Tower, where he had been sent by King Henry because of his suspected involvement in the Pole conspiracy, in which — incidentally — your name was mentioned, Richard.'

'I knew of the plot,' Richard confirmed, 'and it was I who revealed Norfolk's involvement in it to Cromwell. That's why Norfolk plotted to have Cromwell silenced and why I have lived in fear of him all these years. They wished to use me as their figurehead, but I refused.'

'I recall those days, when you were required to hide away at Bradgate,' Grey nodded, 'but you can see how your name, along with Courtney's, would be a great beacon for those who are tired of the Tudor family, who blunder from one dynastic failure to another. Courtney also saw himself as a possible husband for Mary, after the favour she showed him in securing his release, given his staunch Catholicism and his mother's lifelong friendship with Mary. But he is now smarting from his implied rejection as a suitor, and Gardiner has taken his part and is now encouraging him to shower attention on the Lady Elizabeth.'

'You can now readily appreciate why I set my back against continued involvement in Court life.' Richard smiled at Kate by his side. 'It is a veritable snake pit of intrigue and I want none of it. And before you try to remind me once again of who my grandfather is alleged to have been, who else is prepared to act against Mary's marriage to a Spaniard? And who among them can summon an army?'

'Courtney has persuaded Sir Thomas Wyatt of the justice of the cause. Wyatt has a fierce hatred of the Spanish, after what he witnessed of the Inquisition while fighting alongside his father in France. He is a highly respected soldier and is committed to bring two thousand men into any uprising against Philip of Spain becoming Mary's consort.'

'And who else?' Richard persisted.

'Sir James Croft, who served with distinction in Seymour's force during the "Rough Wooing" of Scotland. He has been a lifelong enemy of the Catholic Guise family in France and is concerned that Mary of Scotland may join forces with Philip of Spain once she is also Queen of France. This would leave England under three-way attack. Also Sir Peter Carew, a Devon adventurer and hardened soldier, who also represents Devon in the Parliament, Sir Nicholas Throckmorton, a former ally of Northumberland, Sir Nicholas Arnold, a Parliamentary member for Gloucester who formerly worked for Cromwell and who I believe you once knew, since he speaks highly of you and...'

Richard raised his hand for silence. 'Assuming that you have half the nobility of England behind you, what do you propose?'

'The French Ambassador Antoine de Noailles has promised ships to block any attempt by the Spanish to come to Mary's aid when we depose her in favour of the next in line, Elizabeth, who will then marry Courtenay and release our daughter. She will maintain the Protestant faith and the threat from Spain will be no more.'

'You have already advised the French Ambassador of your plans?' Richard asked, horrified.

Grey smiled. 'Have no fear on that score. He will do anything to score a march over Spain.'

'And the Lady Elizabeth? Has she given her blessing to this?'

'We thought it better not to broach it with her until the rebellion is well under way. She is mightily fearful of Mary, and who can blame the poor lass?'

'And you seek no more from me than the use of my name, for what it is worth?'

'Courtenay would highly value your presence in our victory parade, where you and he may demonstrate to the people of England that the Tudors are not their only option.'

'That will hardly endear us to the Lady Elizabeth.'

'She was a great friend of Jane's during their audiences with Prince Edward when he was a boy and once it is explained to her that Jane only accepted the crown because it was Edward's dying wish, we can talk her round on the ground that one of our motivations was the release from the Tower of her — Elizabeth's — childhood friend who was being unjustly detained there.'

'It's not just Jane,' Kate reminded Richard as she placed her hand gently on the sleeve of his doublet. 'For as long as Jane is held captive, Grace will refuse to leave her side and she will be equally lost to us.'

'You really wish me to add my name — and my neck — to this lunatic scheme?' Richard asked, somewhat taken aback.

'Why should you not?' Kate challenged him. 'You've enjoyed fifteen years of graceful retirement, during which others have risked their lives to keep England peacefully governed. Perhaps it's now your turn.'

XXVII

It went disastrously wrong. The original plan had been for each of the leaders of the rebellion to raise an army in their own locality, in order to converge on London and imprison Mary, replacing her with Elizabeth. But when Imperial Ambassador Simon Renard learned of the presence of French ships in a blocking position in the Channel, he suspected a plot against the throne and alerted England's new Lord Chancellor, Stephen Gardiner. Gardiner had Edward Courtenay arrested.

'You grew too ambitious,' Gardiner explained to Courtenay in his cell in the Tower, to where he had been consigned for questioning and possible torture. 'Your plot was too obvious, given your closeness with the Lady Elizabeth, and I will release you without charge only if you call off your fellow conspirators after you have named them. Do I have your agreement, or do I have to have you racked in order to persuade you to reveal their names?'

Courtenay chose the less painful option, then got word to the others, not only that their plans should proceed no further, due to Gardiner's prior knowledge of them, but that they should look to their own safety, because Gardiner knew their identities.

The unfortunate result of the early discovery of the plot was that the planned uprisings occurred at different times and in isolation, driven by frightened men who had already passed the point of no return. Sir Peter Carew, in Devon, found that the majority of the Protestant nobility were unwilling to draw attention to themselves, given the rumour that Mary was intent on burning anyone who might be suspected of heresy. As for the Catholics in the local community, they had suffered enough for their faith already and were not about to stand in the way of the restoration of the Catholicism for which many of their friends had died. Carew's attempt to recruit a rebel army came to nothing and he was obliged to seek sanctuary across the Channel in Normandy when he was secretly advised that a warrant had been issued for his arrest on a charge of treason.

Of the entire band of conspirators, only Sir Thomas Wyatt proved a threat to Mary. He enjoyed considerable popularity in his native Kent, where rebellion was part of the community's heritage and Protestantism had taken a firm hold. After advancing north in a snowball process that yielded him a total force of some four thousand men, Wyatt got as far as Southwark, where he demanded that the Tower be surrendered to his forces and that Queen Mary be delivered into his custody. This outraged not only the Tower's Lieutenant John Brydges, but almost the entire population on the north bank of the Thames, and when Brydges trained his Tower ordinance on Southwark, Wyatt marched his army to Kingston, approaching London again from the west and along the north bank.

They got as far as Ludgate, where the local citizenry held them back in a skilful series of guerrilla tactics in which they made full use of their superior knowledge of the layout of the backstreets and alleyways so as to demoralise Wyatt's men into deserting in droves. Wyatt surrendered and was consigned to the Tower and its torturers on the express command of Queen Mary, who was determined to obtain information — even if only from a man desperate to end the bodily agony — that Elizabeth had been behind the plot.

Wyatt held firm until he was finally hung, drawn and quartered on Tower Hill by an angry and frustrated Mary, who ordered that Elizabeth be closely confined under what amounted to strict house arrest.

Of the remaining rebels, only Henry Grey, Duke of Suffolk, attempted to put up a fight, with disastrous consequences. He and his wife Frances retreated back to their country estate at Bradgate and began gathering what forces they could among the loyal local populace, including Richard Ashton and a handful of his tenants. The plan was to head south-west, in the belief that enough rebels might still be found in troubled Devon and Cornwall. Had they taken the trouble to learn of the hasty departure from the realm of Sir Peter Carew they would have realised that their cause was already hopeless. As it was, they headed south with less than two hundred fighting men, in the belief that others would answer the call to arms as they progressed.

Richard Ashton spent the night before their departure wrapped in Kate's arms, being reassured that he would be striking a blow for the release of Jane Grey and with her their daughter Grace.

'I know that you regard yourself as a man of peace,' Kate murmured lovingly in Richard's ear, 'but there comes a time when even the meek and mild must take a stance.'

'You see me as meek and mild?' Richard protested.

Kate hugged him harder. 'No, I see you as a man with the courage to do what is necessary to protect those dear to him, and in this you display great bravery. It is easy enough for men of warfare to take up arms, but for those of your loving, peaceful and gracious disposition, it shows even greater courage to take to the field in order to oppose tyranny.'

'You know that I am no soldier,' Richard reminded her, 'and that unless God is with me every step of the way, they will bring me back to Knighton — if at all — across the saddle of my horse?'

'I grieve to think of that,' Kate responded tearfully, 'but even more do I grieve to think of our daughter locked inside the Tower — perhaps even encased in irons — and none lifting a finger to save her. I may not have given birth to Grace, but I love her dearly as my own. Please bring her home, Richard.'

Her pleas were still echoing in his memory as their pathetic force was refused entry to Coventry and Henry Grey opted to surrender rather than lose the lives of his men needlessly in an assault on the town. They were held in the town gaol until John Brydges arrived a week later with a contingent of soldiers from the Tower, in order to convey them south on charges of high treason.

The night before they were due to be loaded into the carts that would take them away to a certain and ignominious death, Richard couldn't sleep. He stirred restlessly in the straw that had been laid on the communal cell floor and tried his best to recall the days in which he had been closer to the workings of the royal mind and had learned Statecraft from his mentor Thomas Cromwell.

It was, so far as he could recall, only following upon a finding, or confession, of guilt of treason, that men were deprived of their estates and their families cast out into the wilderness to starve, or rely on the Christian charity of others. If he could avoid either a trial or the ministrations of the Tower torturer, then Kate and Thomas would not lose Knighton to the royal wrath, regardless of what fate might lie in store for Grace.

But there was only one way he could think of to avoid what undoubtedly lay ahead when they got him to the Tower, and that was his own death before they could reach it. Suicide was a mortal sin, but what if he were to die as part of the aftermath of their recent defeat? Surely God would overlook such a weakness on his part, and had they all not been warned by the Tower Governor, as he yelled at them only that afternoon, that any attempt at escape would result in death?

The following morning, hollow eyed for lack of sleep, the prisoners were led up into the blinding light of a summer morning that forced them all to squint defensively. The prisoners, although bound at the wrists, had been left free to walk to the wagons by the untying of their ankle bonds and they were not roped together. Summoning up every ounce of courage at his command, Richard made a run for it and was therefore able to make a hundred yards start on the guards before they realised what was happening. One of them raised a firearm and took careful aim and Richard landed face down in the dust with a large hole in his back. As his grip on life faded rapidly, he uttered a final silent prayer for his beloved Kate, Grace and Thomas, before it all went black.

Grace placed her arms around Jane and hugged her tightly while they both sobbed their hearts out. Not only were they now confined in a single, cold and barely furnished room with only one bed somewhere in the Bell Tower, immediately behind the bearable chambers they had once occupied in the Lieutenant's House, but they had just been informed by a reluctant Allan that Richard was already dead, having apparently perished during an escape bid, while Henry Grey was to be executed on Tower Hill in the near future and was currently incarcerated in the Bloody Tower that had such an evil reputation.

There was something else that Allan was holding into himself, but which sooner or later he would need to convey to the two girls. Before much longer, Allan would have to reveal that Jane and Guildford were marked for death.

Allan had learned of Mary's wild rage when advised of the involvement of Henry Grey in the Wyatt Rebellion designed to replace her with Elizabeth and free Jane Grey. It was a rage fuelled by fear, Allan speculated, since Mary had been said to have been suspicious of Jane almost from the time of her first arrival as a companion to Edward. Jane had often recounted how Mary had sat glaring while she and Elizabeth had formed a natural friendship, and Allan surmised that she had needed little persuasion that 'the Grey girl' was somehow part of the plot to raise Elizabeth to the throne over her older sister. The Greys were also notorious Protestants and to a suspicious and tortured mind like Mary's this was all that was needed to persuade her that she had been too generous by half to Jane and her husband in not ordering their executions immediately after their trial.

Allan had been instructed that Jane and her 'maidservant' were to be moved from the comparative luxury of their current accommodation immediately after breakfast the previous day, to make way for the Lady Elizabeth. The Bell Tower had been chosen because it was close at hand and had a vacant chamber on the second level. It was also only a short walk from there to Tower Green, where — or so Allan was informed as he tried to keep the shock from his face — Jane would be dispatched on the block immediately after Guildford had been launched into eternity by the same mechanism, but on Tower Hill for the entertainment of the mob.

Allan had suffered the mental torment of seeing Jane and Grace locked behind the heavy oak door of their bleak new surroundings with its barred window that looked over the top of their former residence directly onto Tower Green. He had opted to advise them at that point of the fates of their fathers and had scuttled out of the cell as the howling began, leaving instruction that the prisoners were to be fed once they appeared to be in a fit state to eat.

A further week passed until Allan was told the fateful date — 9th February — and he was about to summon up the courage to tell Jane when he was advised that the date had been put back by three days, for two reasons. The first was in order that Guildford might be executed the same day; and the second was that Mary had given an order that Jane be offered the opportunity to save her soul — if not her neck — by converting to the Catholic faith.

This left Allan with no alternative but to disclose what he knew, in order that Jane could be fully aware of the scheduled attendance upon her of Mary's current personal chaplain, John Feckenham.

Grace looked up at Allan and smiled when he entered the chamber. 'Allan, could you prevail upon our host to inspect our meals before they are sent here? Or even better, to taste them for himself? If we are to starve like this for much longer, we will be dead anyway and the Queen will regret that she showed us mercy in the first place, only to allow us to wither away to nothing. Or is this terrible treatment — hopefully — one more kick before she sets us free? Have you heard something of our impending release, perhaps?'

This had to be the moment, Allan decided, but when he opened his mouth it felt as if his tongue was glued to his upper palate. His eyes bulged slightly, then tears poured down his face and he sank to the floor sobbing pitifully.

Grace rushed over to him and held him upright in her arms. 'I know I smell awful, Allan, but let me hold you. Then tell me what ails you — are you ill?'

Allan tried three times to get the words out, then finally his tongue seemed to loosen itself and out came the dread news he had been keeping to himself for almost a week. 'Oh, dear God, help us all! I … I have to tell you … no, I can't do it. God help me, I can't do it!'

'What is it, Allan?' Grace demanded. 'Have there been more deaths?'

'Not yet … but … but…'

Jane's fate-deadened voice came across the narrow chamber like a church bell tolling for a funeral. 'Is it Guildford?'

Allan nodded and looked pleadingly into Grace's eyes, hoping she could work it out for herself. Suddenly she stiffened and looked blankly back at him as she whispered, 'It's Jane as well, isn't it?'

'Yes,' Allan blurted out. 'On the 12th — next week. Both of them. Guildford on the Hill and Jane on the Green outside.'

XXVIII

A drum beat slowly and regularly, its heavy thud reverberating off the walls and towers of the fortress begun five centuries earlier by a Norman invader. The solemn procession walked to its beat out from under the shaded entrance of the Bell Tower into the bright sunlight of Tower Green, in the centre of which a masked executioner waited, his axe propped up against the block that would receive Lady Jane Grey's neck.

Guildford had already gone ahead of her earlier that morning, in front of a jeering mob on Tower Hill who hadn't really known who he was anyway, only that he was yet another traitor whose very existence was a threat to the newly crowned Queen Mary. As his body had been brought back inside the Tower grounds on a cart, discreetly covered by a cloth and with the head between the knees, Jane had only been able to view it from a distance, which was a mercy, given the amount of blood that had already seeped through the cloth covering.

Jane's procession was led by Allan, by agreement with the Lieutenant, who was delighted to find at least one Captain who didn't shrink from execution escort duties. Immediately behind him was the chaplain who had failed to convert Jane to Catholicism, despite three days of rigorous debate that had at least taken her mind off what lay ahead of her. The man of God had been impressed by her open honesty and the genuineness of her simple faith, while she in turn had found comfort in the man's humanity and gentle grace, and had asked that he be there when she went to meet her Maker.

Next in the pathetically small group came Jane herself, seemingly calm and collected when compared with the quietly sobbing Grace by her side, wishing that she had never been born. She'd needed no additional persuasion when Jane had asked that she accompany her to the block, and nothing on God's earth would prevent her from performing this final service for her lifelong friend. But as she tried to avoid looking at what lay ahead waiting for them in the centre of Tower Green, her mind kept replaying images of two little girls rolling down the grassy bank towards the fishpond, playing at 'prisons' inside the milking parlour, or hiding from Nanny Calthorpe between the birch trees in one of the many small copses on the Bradgate estate. Now they were grown women and it had come to this simply because of who Jane was and the actions of those who couldn't let her be herself, instead of some valuable bargaining piece on a treacherous table.

The procession came to a halt and the executioner stepped forward, as tradition required, and sought her forgiveness. Jane replied in a husky voice that she would forgive him provided that he did what he had to do quickly, and he assured her that he both could and would. As required, Grace handed him the small bag of coins with a shaking hand, and Allan leaned between them with the blindfold.

'Where do I go?' Jane asked in a barely audible whisper.

The executioner nodded towards the wooden block, smeared brown with the indelible evidence of previous use.

Allan whispered to Grace that she would need to apply the blindfold, and with shaking hands Grace placed it over Jane's eyes and began her attempt to tie it. But she was trembling so violently that her shaking hands couldn't form the knot, so Jane reached calmly behind her and tied it herself. Then she walked a few paces forward with her arms outstretched like a sleepwalker and stopped.

'Where's the block?' she asked.

Allan stepped from behind them, took her arm gently and led her to a position in front of the ominous lump of wood. Then he assisted her into a kneeling position and once again she reached out gropingly into the open air in front of her.

'Lower,' Grace told her in a choking whisper and finally Jane's hand came into contact with the block.

Once she was positioned, the executioner picked up the axe that had been resting on the side of the block and indicated with a gesture of his head that everyone should step back. Allan led Grace gently back a few paces, then deliberately turned her head round and muffled it against his shoulder.

There was a flash of metal in the bright sunlight and then a swishing sound, followed by a squelching thud and Grace collapsed in a dead faint into Allan's waiting arms.

Grace came around as they were carrying her back into the chamber she had shared with Jane, and her first action was to call out for Allan. As his face appeared in front of hers with a look of deep concern, she asked if she had just awoken from a bad dream.

'I'm afraid not,' he replied. 'It really happened.'

'So Jane's dead?'

'Yes.'

'God rest her soul.' Grace said, then gave herself over to heartbroken sobs as Allan rocked her gently in his arms. After a while she stopped and looked around her. 'Is this the chamber I shared with Jane?'

'Yes,' Allan replied, steeling himself for what had to come next.

'Did you bring me here because I fainted?'

'Yes.'

'When can I go home?' When it fell silent, Grace gripped his arm fearfully. 'Am I next?'

'Not so far as I know, but my orders are that you're to be held here awaiting further command from the Queen.'

'But she can't suspect me of anything, surely?'

'Who knows? They say she's raving mad.'

'Will you still be able to be my guard, even though I'm not as important as Jane was?'

'You are to me,' Allan reassured her as he leaned forward to kiss her.

XXIX

Allan continued to call regularly, during his off-duty hours, at the Grey house in The Minories, where those who remained of the Dudley and Grey families still met in their mutual misery in what had become an almost unthinking ritual as one tragedy followed another. There were now two widows — Jane Dudley and Kate Ashton — sharing a chamber on the upper floor and recently joining them around the supper table as they tried their best to eat in order to keep up their flagging spirits was Frances Grey, tearfully awaiting a date for husband Henry's execution. There was also the gloomy prospect that once Henry Grey was executed, his estates would be forfeit to the Crown and they would all be seeking somewhere to begin what was left of the rest of their lives.

Kate Ashton was hopeful that since Richard had never been attainted with a charge of treason, and had not lived long enough to be tortured into confessing it, they might all find temporary sanctuary on the modest estate of Knighton, and in this they were being encouraged by the seemingly inexhaustible Mary Calthorpe, in her seventy-second year, as physically fragile as a sparrow, but with an indomitable spirit born of an unflagging faith in the mercy of the God she would soon be allowed to worship in the way she had practised while in holy orders.

It was Mary who ordered the servants around, Mary who commissioned food from tradesmen for as long as the Grey credit remained good, and Mary who insisted that they eat at least one meal a day, 'to the glory of God', as she justified it. It was also Mary who seemed to sag when told by a downcast

Allan that Grace was still being held in the Tower on unspecified charges and that 'the mad old bitch' Queen Mary seemed determined to make executions on Tower Hill a daily form of entertainment for the mob.

'But the poor wee lamb hasn't done nothing except be a friend to poor Jane, God rest her soul,' Mary protested as she made the sign of the cross across the threadbare smock that encased her bony chest.

'Any friend of Jane's seems to be suspect,' Allan explained, 'and if the Lieutenant finds out that Grace is my intended, I'll be next on the list.'

'So there's no way you can get her out of there?' Mary asked.

Allan shook his head.

'Can't you just walk her out of there, pretending as how she's been set free?'

'I wouldn't get past the Middle Tower without release papers signed by the Lieutenant,' Allan explained, 'and this is probably not the best time to be admitting that I can't read or write.'

'So how can you get them release papers?' Mary asked, as if they might be conjured up with a wave of the hand.

'No idea, unless you can persuade that mad bitch of a Queen to sign them,' Allan replied with a shake of the head.

A gleam appeared in Mary's eye. 'She may be mad, but she fears God,' was her reply as Allan took his weary departure.

Three days later, the usher inside the Audience Chamber at Greenwich Palace approached the Queen warily and stood there silently until she looked up from her prayer book with an irritated expression.

'Well?'

'Begging your pardon, Your Majesty, but there's an elderly person been seeking audience with you for two days now. We tried to shoo her away, but she took root in the scullery and she's threatening to die in there unless she gets to speak with you. By the look of her, that won't be much longer anyway, so perhaps if you don't want a dead body in your scullery...'

'Who is she?' Mary demanded.

The usher shrugged his head. 'No idea, except she claims to have met your mother at some time in her life. She said to tell you that she was once "Mother Maria Magdelena" of Knighton Convent and that she has important information regarding a prisoner in the Tower.'

Intrigued, Mary waved her hand in a gesture for the person to be admitted and five minutes later a very feeble looking Mary Calthorpe was ushered into the presence, where she executed a wobbly curtsey as she held on to a vacant chair for support, then asked permission to be allowed to sit in it.

'What business brings you here?' the Queen demanded as she nodded for the old lady to sit.

Mary Calthorpe began the speech she had spent three days rehearsing. 'I've come to plead for the release of a harmless girl who hasn't done anyone any harm in her life, Your Majesty, and whose father was the means by which former holy sisters were allowed to carry on, even after that evil Master Cromwell had done his dirty work.'

'I'm informed that you were once a nun — is that correct?' Queen Mary asked, reluctant to believe that this rambling skeletal wreck of a woman was ever so well established in life, but intrigued to learn of the possibility that some holy house had survived the Dissolution that had been so thorough and relentless.

'Yes indeed, Your Majesty — "Mother Maria Magdelena" I was once, after the previous Holy Mother died and the other nuns chose me. Benedictines we were, in a house founded by your own pious and blessed mother.'

'She founded so many,' Mary told her, 'that I never knew them all.'

'But you were there once, Your Majesty. You won't remember, since you were only a wee bubby in your mother's arms, and I was one of those who gave you a blessing. Your father was mighty pleased, as I recall.'

'My mother and my father?' Queen Mary asked, thoroughly absorbed by a glimpse of the distant past, before any of the heartbreak she had seen her mother suffer. 'Where was this, exactly?'

'A place called Knighton, Your Majesty — just north of Leicester. The convent was ordered to close, but the wonderful man who was given the estate on which it was placed gave us permission to carry on our good works, and still under our vows, except we weren't allowed to dress like nuns anymore, in case Cromwell found out.'

'He sounds like a very worthy man — does he accompany you to Court?'

'No, Your Majesty, he died a short while ago,' Mary replied, seeking God's forgiveness for the white lie involved in not mentioning precisely how he came to die, 'but it's his daughter who is still locked up in the Tower, and she's every bit as virtuous and God-fearing as him, and all she did was serve the Lady Jane.'

'You mean Jane Grey?'

'Yes, Your Majesty. I were fortunate enough to be nanny to both of them at the same time, and they grew up together on the Grey estate of Bradgate. A right pair of little mischiefs they were and no mistake, but only "little girl" naughtiness and so far as Grace's concerned, there wasn't ever a drop of bad in her, honest to God.'

'How did she come to be in league with Jane Grey?' Mary demanded suspiciously.

'She wasn't "in league" with her, except in the way that little girls can be such good friends, like these two were. They were inseparable and when Jane got made Queen she asked Grace to be one of her ladies-in-waiting and that was all there was in it, so help me God. She doesn't mean you any badness, Your Majesty, and she just wants to marry her intended and become the wife of a farrier in Nottinghamshire. I'll take an oath on the Bible on that, if you wish, only you're the only one I know of who can set her free.'

'What was her name again?' Mary asked. 'It was "Grace" something or other, was it not?'

'Yes, Your Majesty — "Grace Ashton".'

'Very well.' Mary rang the small handbell on the table beside her and when the attendant responded to her call she demanded vellum, quill and ink.

Ten minutes later, Mary Calthorpe left the Palace clutching a small document under the safety of her borrowed cloak and with a broad grin on her weathered face as she muttered in triumph, 'You may be all growed up now, Grace Ashton, but you still need your old Nanny Calthorpe.'

XXX

Ten days later, a small group of weary travellers appeared on the road from Leicester and an excited shout did the rounds of the retainers on the Knighton estate. Domestic staff hurried to sweep clean the almost abandoned kitchen, while fires were lit in all the rooms and windows were thrown open to provide an exit for the dust that rose from the old rushes that were being hastily replaced.

'Welcome back, Mistress!' was the universal welcome as Kate Ashton led the way indoors and introduced the visitors to the family Steward.

'This is Lady Frances, from the Grey estate further north, James, and the lady on her left is Jane Dudley, Dowager Duchess of Northumberland. They will be residing here until further notice and they may share my old chambers on the next level. I'll have Mistress Grace's old room, and where exactly has Master Thomas got to?'

'He's out riding somewhere, Mistress. Might I enquire after Mistress Grace and Mistress Mary Calthorpe?'

'They took the direct road to Nottingham, rather than divert to call in here. Mistress Grace is to be married near there and she's accompanied by Mary Calthorpe and her husband to be.'

'Very good, Mistress. Might I say again how good it is to have you back here? I hope as how you intend to stay for good, now you're back?'

'I most certainly do, James, although there may come a time when I have to journey north for christenings.'

'Let me guess,' Grace bubbled with happiness as she was

introduced to the rest of the Bestwick family, 'you must be Amy.'

The older of the two girls nodded from above the bulging stomach that housed her eagerly anticipated firstborn.

'Then that makes you Amos, doesn't it?' she asked the towering lump who was almost Allan's double, if twice his width. When Amos nodded, Grace looked down with mock seriousness at the tiny girl who was gazing up at her with wide brown eyes. 'Nell?'

The little girl nodded, then giggled and hid her face in her mother's apron.

Grace looked studiously at the remaining two boys. 'I can't tell Tom from Jack, I'm afraid.'

'I'm Tom,' said the more forward of the two, 'an' the daft lookin' wun's Jack.'

They took to their customary wrestling, until their father pulled them apart and apologised.

'Sorry, Mistress, but they gets a bit lively wi' strangers. 'Cept yer ain't gunner be a stranger much longer, is yer?'

'Indeed not,' Allan confirmed and Grace was suddenly aware that somehow, somewhere, Allan had lost the rough local dialect that must have been his during his childhood, to judge by the way his brothers and sisters spoke. 'Say "hello" to the next Mrs Bestwick, once the Reverend Morley has a spare day,' he added.

'Hello,' they chimed in unison.

Allan's father Edward nodded towards Mary Calthorpe. 'Is this lady your intended mother-in-law, son?'

'No, she's my nanny,' Grace explained. 'It's a long story,' she added when she saw the puzzled looks from her new family.

A month after their arrival, Allan and Grace slipped outside to avoid the rising din of fiddle playing and dancing as the celebrations following the wedding feast climbed to an ear-threatening level. At the far end of the rambling garden they sat down once again on the crude bench on which they'd spent hours planning their immediate future. Now their future had arrived and earlier that day they had tied the knot in the parish church of St Mary's, three doors up from the Bestwick forge.

'What will happen to you if they catch you?' Grace asked fearfully.

Allan smiled as he leaned forward and kissed her on the lips. 'I wouldn't be the first Yeoman to desert,' he told her, 'and at the rate that they're conducting executions inside there, they won't have time to search for me in Attenborough.'

'I still can't believe that Nanny Calthorpe had that much influence over the Queen.'

'She was once the head of a convent, wasn't she?' Allan reminded her. 'They say that Queen Mary's terrified of going to Hell.'

'And yet she commits so many sins, executing innocent people,' Grace shuddered. 'Is it true that Archbishop Cranmer and two others are to be burned at the stake?'

'Let's talk about something else,' Allan urged her. 'Like whether or not you're going to be bored living here when we've finished building our own house.'

'Not at all,' Grace assured him, finally feeling at peace.

A NOTE TO THE READER

Dear Reader,

Thank you for joining me through the maelstrom of the most turbulent period of the Tudor era, during which England had four monarchs in the space of seven years, including the hapless Jane Grey who is a central figure in this novel and whose throne life barely exceeded a week.

Historians have argued ever since over the extent to which she was a victim of the ambitions of others, and I opted to underline the inevitability of her downfall by comparing her actual life with the life that might have been, by creating her fictitious lifelong friend, the even more naive Grace Ashton. The tragedy of Jane's life leaps out from the page by contrasting Grace's 'ordinary' life with that of the hapless Jane, thrust unwillingly into Court politics as the pawn of others.

From two little girls rolling and giggling in the muddy grass of Bradgate, we follow their fortunes to the heart-wrenching spectacle of Grace standing, broken-hearted, alongside Jane in the final moment before the executioner's axe falls.

As usual, I have made full use of the known facts from this period and most notably the arrogant stupidity of the Seymour brothers, Thomas and Edward. Following the death of Henry VIII, the English crown lay in a vacuum, with a nine-year-old boy ruling through a Council during the upheavals of religious reform, agricultural revolution, troubled relationships with France and Spain and the ever-present threat from the Scottish border. Edward VI relied — too heavily — on his two Seymour uncles, both of whom fell spectacularly from grace due to over-weaning ambition.

Thomas recovered from the disgrace of marrying Henry's last Queen, Catherine Parr, but really did expose himself to the ire of not only the boy King, but also his straight-laced half-sister Mary, by engaging in bedroom romps with the remaining half-sister, the fourteen-year-old Elizabeth. He also really did go one step too far when, for reasons of his own, he was caught, armed to the teeth, in an apparent attempt on the life of King Edward, during the course of which he shot dead the favourite royal dog.

As if determined to prove that lack of brainpower was a Seymour legacy, his brother Edward really did make a virtual prisoner of King Edward at Windsor Castle. His downfall was the cue for the rise to royal preferment of another whose ambitions were to be the rock upon which Jane Grey would be shipwrecked, the devious John Dudley, Duke of Northumberland, who appears to have been privy to King Edward's wish to devolve the crown on Jane and took steps to ensure that when this happened, his son Guildford would be the Queen's Consort, if not actually King.

Another arguing point for historians has been why the fifteen-year-old Edward left the crown in his will to a distant relative from Leicestershire, in defiance of the progression legislation enacted during the reign of his father, which prescribed that Mary and her heirs should succeed, followed by Elizabeth and hers. Was it simply because Edward saw in Jane the best prospect for continuing the Protestant religious reform begun by Henry and ardently pursued by Edward? If so, then surely Elizabeth would have been a safer bet, since — as she went on to prove, despite the risks that she thereby ran — the younger sister was also determined that the 'old' Catholic observances would be a thing of the past.

Or could it have been more personal? It does not stretch the known facts too far to suggest that Edward had conceived a pubescent fancy for his refreshingly open and naive second cousin and saw in her a reflection of what he might have been, had it not been for the circumstances of his birth. Likewise, Jane herself would discover to her cost that being born to a royal niece came with a massive price tag in terms of being allowed to live life as one chose.

There are certainly enough dramatic incidents to be observed during this period to make the task of an historical novelist seeking to recreate it an easy one, without bending the truth to breaking point. I hope that you found the end product satisfying to read, but I have not yet finished with either the Ashton family or the other young lady caught up in this Courtly whirlwind, young Elizabeth Tudor. In the next novel in the series, *The Queen in Waiting*, we watch from the safety of the side-lines as Elizabeth struggles to maintain both her reputation and her head.

As ever, I look forward to receiving feedback from you, whether in the form of a review on **Amazon** or **Goodreads**. Or, of course, you can try the more personal approach on my website and my Facebook page: **DavidFieldAuthor**.

Happy reading!

David

davidfieldauthor.com

Sapere Books is an exciting new publisher of brilliant fiction and popular history.

To find out more about our latest releases and our monthly bargain books visit our website:
saperebooks.com

Printed in Great Britain
by Amazon